Discover the heart and faith of a true legend—
a tale of love, loss, and the strength to endure.

TRUE LEGEND

The Story of Ezra Mulvey

MARK GENGLER

Titles by Mark Gengler

THANKS A LOT, GOD

– OUR ANCESTORS SERIES –

NOAH THORNE
A WISCONSIN FARM BOY IN THE 1920'S

WOLF CREEK CIDER
THE STORY OF AARON STROUD

MIGRANT!
THE STORY OF DANNY BROOME

MARSHFIELD 1919
THE STORY OF WAYNE SCHOOLEY

ORPHAN
THE STORY OF TYLER BRAUN

TRUE LEGEND
THE STORY OF EZRA MULVEY

Discover the heart and faith of a true legend—
a tale of love, loss, and the strength to endure.

TRUE LEGEND

The Story of Ezra Mulvey

MARK GENGLER

SOUL FIRE PRESS

TRUE LEGEND *The Story of Ezra Mulvey*
by Mark Gengler
Our Ancestors series

Published by

SOUL FIRE PRESS
an imprint of First Steps Publishing
PO Box 571 • Gleneden Beach, OR 97388
FirstStepsPublishing.com

Interior layout, cover design by Suzanne Parrott
Cover art *Gina's Valley* © 2024 Suzanne Parrott
  Illustration created using Midjourney

Young Adult, 1920s, Early 20th Century historical fiction, Wisconsin, rural life, romance, heroism, love, friendship

ISBN: 978-1-945146-59-6 (pb)
         978-1-945146-60-2 (epub)

10 9 8 7 6 5 4 3 2 1

Printed in the
United States of America

This novel is dedicated to my late brother, Peter Gengler. Pete was two years older and my best friend through our growing years. We had many good times and some hard times in our youth, but we made the best of them.

Pete taught me to love the outdoors, fishing, and hunting. We planted and weeded the garden in spring and summer and picked berries together each fall. We milked cows, loaded hay wagons with bales, and made firewood for winter. I seldom saw Pete lose his temper. He took things in stride.

As a boy, he loved baseball – his favorite team was the Brooklyn Dodgers. He collected all their baseball cards. He played ball for two years with the Rudolph High School ball team.

To this day, I miss him.

Thank you, Pete.

"No one has ever become poor by giving."
— Anne Frank

"The best way to find yourself
is to lose yourself in the service of others."
— Mahatma Gandhi

CHAPTER ONE

An early spring morning in May. Sitting on the wooden bench outside his cabin, Ezra Mulvey tasted the strong coffee from the granite-ware mug. The air was cool but not cold. It would be a warm day, with a rain shower in late evening. Scratching his chin, he realized it had been days since he shaved last. 'A bath wouldn't hurt either,' he thought. A chickadee perched on the arm of the bench, tipping its dark head from side to side as it looked him over. Slowly, Ezra extended his left arm out, palm down. The little bird hopped onto his hand, walked up his arm, and perched on his shoulder. Smiling, Ezra sipped his coffee and planned his day.

Ezra was born in 1889 in a trapper's cabin on the bank of Walnut Creek in northern Wisconsin. The Cree midwife who assisted his mother spoke only a few words of English but knew her trade well. Ezra's pa, Bertram, arrived back at the cabin days later. He had been making his last trip to pick up his traps for the year. Bert wrote down the month of April and the year 1889. Neither he nor his wife had any idea what day the birth had occurred. Two years later, a younger brother, Micah, was born in another cabin somewhere in Price County. The date was June 1891.

Bertram was a trapper in fall and winter and worked any odd job he could find the rest of the year. When the leaves began to fall, and the first frost arrived, Bert moved the family to another area he had scouted that summer. Bert's wife, Flower, was half Cree and half French. She went where her husband took her and the children. She had few possessions, one of which was an old McGuffy's reader, given to her by a traveling minister. In this, she kept the two birth notes of her sons.

In 1896, Flower, tired of life as a trapper's wife, decided to return to her people. She waited until Bert was running his trapline, then gave the book to five-year-old Ezra, kissed her sons goodbye, and walked out of their life. When Bert returned a week later, he shrugged his shoulders, told Ezra, "Look after your brother," and went back to trapping.

In the fall of 1895, gold was found in the Klondike. The news reached Seattle, Washington in the summer of 1896. The newspapers spread the news, and by the spring of 1897, the entire country was struck with gold fever. Bert Mulvey decided to go to Alaska but knew it was no place for children.

He bought a section of wooded property using the money saved from trapping. With the help of his sons and a workhorse, he built a log cabin. Bunks were crafted and a stove was installed. Water came from a creek just 20 yards away. Cutting an adequate supply of firewood, Bert told Ezra, "Take care of Micah. I'll be back when I strike it rich." Bert left behind his .30-.30 Winchester rifle and an Ithaca .410 shotgun. With only his .45 Colt pistol, he left Wisconsin for the Klondike gold fields in the summer of 1901.

Ezra and Micah were both excellent shots, and small game was plentiful. A garden had been planted and yielded potatoes, carrots, onions, and squash. Using Bert's traps, the boys set out their first trapline. Through trial and error, they trapped a muskrat, a marten, a mink, and a lynx, which was a prize catch. By spring, Ezra and Micah had some fine pelts for their efforts. Loading up the old workhorse, they took their bounty to the general store and trading post at the crossroads, run by Cyrus and Inez Thorne.

Cyrus gave the two boys some sound advice. "Your pelts will earn you $102," he said. "It would be wise to keep the money here and open an account. Each time you make a purchase, I will charge your account and tell you how much you have remaining." Ezra and Micah agreed.

School at the Crossroads began in September, and Ezra enrolled Micah. It took two wrestling matches, both of which Ezra won, to convince Micah to go to school. Once there, Micah learned to read and write. In the evenings, the younger boy taught the older to do the same. Micah's quick mind absorbed history, basic math, and geography. Ezra was content with reading and writing.

In the winter of 1903, the old workhorse died. Fourteen-year-old Ezra walked to the Crossroads general store and informed Cyrus, "I need another horse."

Cyrus quite often traded cows and horses with the locals. "I think I have a horse you might like," he told Ezra. From the stable behind the store, Cyrus led out a chestnut workhorse. "This gelding is six years old and trained for harness or saddle. I took it in trade for a past-due bill. He is yours for $50."

Ezra looked at the horse and liked what he saw. "Do I have enough in my account to buy him?"

"You have $75 in your account," Cyrus told him, "and I will throw in an old saddle." With the deal struck, Cyrus showed Ezra how to saddle a horse and watched as he rode away.

Back in the store, Cyrus told Inez about the sale. "That horse could have brought you $100 in the spring," she said with a raised eyebrow.

With a slight grin and a wave of his hand, Cyrus replied, "I'm way ahead if I don't have to feed that horse until spring." Inez knew that Cyrus had a soft spot in his heart for the Mulvey boys, just as she did.

"Thank you," she whispered as she kissed Cyrus's cheek. "Heaven will be your reward."

The garden was planted each spring, and another furrow was added each year. Ezra planted something new every year to add variety to their meals. Sweet corn and tomatoes were big hits. Green beans and peas became a staple both boys liked. Nature provided the meat for their table: grouse, rabbits, squirrels, fish, and venison in the fall and winter. At age 14, Ezra was a man – built tall and rangy like his father. Micah was shorter but husky and strong. Both were dark-haired and brown-eyed, a trait inherited from their mother.

Ezra was not a talker unless it was people he knew and trusted. Micah was a chatterbox, often to the annoyance of his brother. With a quick mind and deft fingers, he could fix almost anything. One fall morning, Ezra woke to find Micah working at the table by lamplight. Spread out before him was the Winchester rifle, its inner workings laid out in a pattern on a cloth.

"I'll need that rifle today, Micah," Ezra said.

"The action was sticking," Micah told him. "It needs a good cleaning and oiling. I'll have it back together soon."

Ezra brought in some wood, put the coffee on, and warmed up last night's rabbit stew while watching Micah work. Before the assembly began, each small part was checked, cleaned, and oiled. 'It's like watching a magic show,' thought Ezra. Then it was done.

Handing the rifle to his brother, Micah said, "Take it outside and try it."

Bang! Bang! Bang!

Ezra was amazed! The action was now smooth as silk. "Works perfect," he told Micah. "Now eat your stew; we got a trapline to run."

The following summer, Ezra ran a pipeline from the creek to the cabin. Digging beneath the frost line, he laid the pipe and cut a hole through the cabin floor to slide the pipe through. He got the sink and hand pump from Cyrus at the store. After some priming, the clear water gushed from the pump. No more breaking the ice on the creek on a January morning to get water. The old lean-to for the horse was falling down, so they took it apart, cut up the old logs for firewood, and built a new structure with more room for hay to last through the winter. It was a hard life, but it made strong men. Ezra and Micah Mulvey were proving they were up to the challenge.

CHAPTER TWO

Through their dealings with Cyrus at the store, Ezra and Micah got to know the Thorne family. There were three sons: Nathan, Eban, and Foley. Nathan had a head for business and would take over the Crossroads general store when Cyrus retired. Eban liked the farming life and worked for most of the local farmers at one time or another. Foley spent all his spare time at the blacksmith shop, learning the trade.

Of all the men he knew, Ezra liked and respected one above the others. Conner Lundtz was a logging boss for the Shipman Lumber Company during the winter and built barns for a living the rest of the year. Ezra found work with Conner, who had hired Bert Mulvey at times. Conner treated Ezra as a man, and Ezra responded in kind, giving a day's work for a day's pay. Conner understood that Ezra's wages went to Cyrus at the store, and he approved. 'Too often, young men and their money are soon parted,' Conner thought, and helped Ezra when he could.

Micah had taken to gardening, planting, and caring for the growing plants. He convinced Ezra that they needed a cookstove, not just the stove they used for heating. Grudgingly, Ezra agreed. Young Nathan delivered the stove by wagon and then helped to bring it in and set it up. Soon, with the help of a cookbook Inez gave him, Micah was preparing meals, baking pies, and even baking loaves of bread!

"You will make some woman a fine husband," Ezra said with a smile.

It was 1905 when Ezra was called upon to help the local sheriff. It was a late summer afternoon, and Ezra was cutting logs into firewood for the coming winter. Sheriff Albert Holmes drove into the Mulvey's yard in a one-horse spring wagon. Albert was in his late 40s, medium tall, spare of build, and weathered from hours spent outdoors. Stepping down from the wagon, he approached Ezra, and they shook hands. "I need your help," he stated bluntly. "I've got two lost children. The family stopped for lunch by the meadow at Bryce Creek, about 5 miles past the Crossroads toward Burkesville. The children, a boy and a girl, ages 10 and 12, were playing with their dog. The dog took off after a rabbit, and the kids chased after it. Do you think you could track them down?" Sinking his axe into the chopping block, Ezra said, "You head back, keep the parents calm, and I'll saddle up and follow."

The track was challenging to follow in the dry grass and brush. The sun was beginning to set when Ezra reached the tree line, and he stopped often to listen. About 200 yards into the woods, he heard the faint voices coming from ahead. The two frightened children sat in a small clearing, holding the dog. Stepping slowly down from his horse, he said, "How would you two like a horseback ride back to your folks?" Taking a length of rope from his saddlebag, he tied it loosely around the dog's neck. He lifted the children onto the horse and began the long walk back, leading the horse and dog.

The weekly newspaper from Burkesville ran a story about the rescue. It briefly mentioned Ezra by name. The sheriff offered to pay Ezra for his time, but Ezra refused. "I don't charge for helping folks," was his remark. A rumor began circulating that the Mulveys built a still and cooked moonshine. Neither Ezra nor Micah had a taste for raw liquor, but the rumor persisted. Ezra caught two of the Hatch boys on his property one night, looking for the still. Both were soundly thrashed and warned against ever trying it again.

In 1908, Ezra trapped his first beaver. A prosperous local farmer, Hiram Kruetzer, left word at the Crossroads store that he needed help from Ezra. Riding out to the Kruetzer farm, Ezra noticed the lower end of a hayfield underwater. Hiram was waiting for Ezra at the house. "A family of beavers has built a dam on Bryce Creek, and I need them trapped out," he said. "How much will you charge me for that?"

"Nothing," Ezra told him. "What I get for the pelts is enough." Ezra rode along the creek until he spotted the dam. The dome of a beaver house was poking out of the water. 'Got to talk to Micah about this,' he thought.

That night, after supper, the two sat down with one of Micah's books and read up on beavers. By the end of the week, two beavers, a male and a female, were caught. The dam was broken up, and the beaver house was torn down. The hides only brought $5 apiece, but Cyrus had some new information for Ezra.

"I got a letter recently from a company interested in wild ginseng. If you know of any, the roots are bringing in $25 an ounce, thoroughly dried." With a slight smile, Ezra said, "I might know where there is a plant or two."

From Flower, his mother, Ezra had learned of the healing powers of the ginseng root. Ground to a fine powder, the plant's root was effective against upset stomachs, the common cold, and lessening the flu virus. The plant sported a tiny red berry. When planted, the seed within the berry grew more plants.

Ezra and Micah had their small plot of ginseng hidden deep within the forest. Several roots were now drying in the cabin, hung from the rafters. Collecting them, Ezra wrapped them in a cloth and took them to Cyrus.

Weighing them out, Cyrus gave a slow, soft whistle. "Just a hair over eight ounces," he said. "I'll let the company know, and someone will be out to pick these up."

Two weeks later, Cyrus showed Ezra a bill of sale for $225. "Just credit my account," Ezra said with a smile.

CHAPTER THREE

On the 28th of June, 1914, Archduke Ferdinand and his wife Sophia were shot and killed by a young Serb revolutionary. It was a major international story but carried only briefly in local newspapers. "Those crazy Europeans are always making trouble," one farmer told another at the Crossroads store. "Glad it don't involve us," was the response.

Soon, every nation overseas was taking sides. Ferdinand was the heir of Franz-Joseph, Emperor of the Austria-Hungary Empire, and a distant relative of Kaiser Wilhelm of Germany. When the dust settled in 1916, it was clear there would be a war to end all wars. America's President, Woodrow Wilson, vowed to keep the United States out of the conflict. However, on April 6th, 1917, America's government declared war on Germany.

Micah Mulvey was packing his bag. "I am meeting Eban Thorne and three other guys at the Crossroads," he told Ezra. "Cyrus is driving us into Burkesville to join the Army."

"This ain't your fight," Ezra told him. "Let them foreigners fight it out among themselves."

"I can't stand by while the rest of the world is at war," Micah said. "I need to do my part."

Ezra slowly shook his head, realizing his younger brother

was a man who made his own decisions. "I will write as often as I can," Micah said, holding out his hand. For a long moment, the brothers clasped hands as they looked into each other's eyes. Then, with a smile and a wave, Micah was gone.

The Burkesville volunteers trained at Camp McCoy and were soon formed into the 16th Infantry Regiment with units from Minnesota and Iowa. Their next stop was Camp Gordon, Georgia. Micah's letters told of the heat, red clay, and Southern cooking.

"They got a plant here called okra," he wrote. "They use it like we use potatoes, but it tastes awful." He described the new rifles the Army issued to soldiers. "It's a bolt action 1903 model Springfield in .30-.06 caliber and holds five rounds in the magazine. I put all five shots in the bullseye and got a sharpshooter medal."

Ezra smiled and thought, 'I hope he doesn't take it apart some night to see how it works.'

A letter usually arrived every two weeks, and Ezra would answer maybe once a month. He followed the stories in the newspaper Cyrus would save for him. It seemed the German army was on the move, headed for France. The French dug in along the border in trenches, and the Germans did the same. In between was 'no man's land,' and the artillery fire from both sides would go on for hours.

'Hell of a way to fight a war,' Ezra thought.

Like most summers, Ezra worked for Conner Lundtz, building a barn. Ezra was good friends with Conner's son, Gilbert, and they often had lunch together.

How is Micah enjoying the army life?" Gilbert asked.

"He likes going on hikes and shooting at the rifle range,"

Ezra said, "but the marching and close-order drills are not to his liking."

"I've been thinking about joining the Navy," Gilbert said.

Ezra gave his friend a sideways look. "How does Conner feel about that?"

"I haven't told him yet. I don't think he or Ma would be too happy about it."

"Let me know what you decide to do, Gilbert," said Ezra. "As for me, I'm staying put."

It was a sultry Friday – the end of a hot, humid week. Ezra and Nathan sat on the general store porch catching up on the local news over a cold bottle of beer when an old Model-T with steam drifting up from the radiator eased into the drive. A man wearing work clothes and a battered derby hat climbed down, walked to the passenger side, and helped his wife from the car. From the backseat, a boy, about 16, jumped out, followed by a dark-haired girl, about 18, wearing a print dress.

Nathan's beer stopped halfway to his mouth as he stared at the girl. Ezra noticed and smiled but said nothing.

The man smiled as he walked up the steps and removed his hat. "Hello. I'm Sean O'Riley. My family and I are on our way to Minnesota, but our Ford overheated again. Might I trouble you for some water?"

Slowly putting down his beer, Nathan stood. "There's a bucket by the pump. Help yourself."

"I thank you, sir," said Sean. "Let me introduce my family: my wife Beth, our son Patrick, and our daughter Rose. Patrick, fill the bucket."

Cyrus came out of the store after hearing the conversation.

"Why not spend the night here, let the car cool off, and continue in the morning?" Cyrus offered the family.

Nathan could not take his eyes off Rose, who seemed likewise afflicted.

Ezra chuckled as he watched the transfixed couple. He smiled broadly, mounted his horse at the hitch rail, and rode home.

The following Thursday, Nathan knocked on Ezra's door.

"Coffee is on; come on in," Ezra said.

Nathan entered and sat down. Not one to waste words, he exclaimed, "Rose and I are getting married on Saturday at the church. I want you there."

Pouring the coffee, Ezra smiled. "Kinda sudden, isn't it?"

Blushing, Nathan shook his head. "Maybe, but we are in love, and she wants to stay here–with me."

Ezra sat down and took a sip of coffee. "When I saw the two of you looking at each other, I knew she would never see Minnesota."

Nathan smiled and started laughing, which caused Ezra to laugh! When the laughing died down, Nathan said, "Foley will be my best man, but you are my best friend. I want you to be there."

"What time?"

"Ten o'clock," Nathan answered. "No need to dress up."

"Well, I might shave," Ezra said with a smile.

In January 1918, the U.S. Army decided it had trained enough soldiers for war; now, it was time to get them to

France. It took another two months to find the ships to carry the troops and two more months to refit the transports to house and feed thousands of soldiers. The first group of ships left port in late June 1918.

Micah wrote Ezra just before they sailed. "The ship I will leave on is the USS *Saratoga*," he said. We are finally on our way to France. I hope I don't get seasick."

On the foggy morning of June 14th, a convoy of ships left New York harbor. Along with the troop ships were two fuel tankers, freighters, destroyers, cargo ships, and two armed yachts as escorts. More ships would follow within days. The weather was good, and the first ships reached France on June 26th.

Micah wrote, "We arrived in France yesterday and spent the time unloading cargo we would need to get to the front lines. I will write more later." Ezra shared the news with the Thorne family at the store.

"Eban was on one of the cargo ships helping with the horses," Cyrus said. "He always was good with horses."

Ezra had his first real visit with Rose, and her straightforward manner was welcome. "You must visit more often," she said. "Nathan looks upon you as family."

News came that Sheriff Albert Holmes had decided to retire. "I will not be on the ballot again," he told everyone, "but Deputy Luther Godfrey would make a good sheriff."

Luther was 27 years old and had been a deputy for four years. He knew his job, and folks trusted him. With Albert Holmes' recommendation, Luther was elected. A few weeks later, he paid Ezra a visit.

"I know you don't vote," he said, "but I hope I can count on you if I need you."

"This time, I *did* vote," Ezra said. "I wanted you to have the job. We know each other and get along. If you need me, let me know."

Cyrus Thorne's wife, Inez, had a stroke and died. She and Rose had been stocking shelves with canned goods when she suddenly turned pale, gasped, "Oh my lord," and collapsed on the floor.

"Nathan, help me!" Rose screamed. Cyrus and Nathan came running in. Nathan lifted his mother from the floor and carried her to the bedroom, but it was too late. Her heart had stopped.

The funeral was two days later.

Cyrus was in a fog, just going through the motions. Nathan and Rose handled the proceedings, managing everything that needed to be done when a beloved family member passed.

At the grave site, when her body was lowered into the grave, tears dripped from Nathan's eyes. Rose held onto her husband to support him. Cyrus wept and staggered slightly. His son Foley held his right arm, and Ezra Mulvey held his left. Later, back at the church, the women of the Parrish had set up a luncheon. Stories were told, and good times were remembered.

Then, Ezra, saying goodbye to the Thorne family, rode slowly home.

CHAPTER FOUR

'October just might be my favorite month,' thought Ezra. It was sunrise; no frost yet, but it wouldn't be long coming. The temperatures dipped into the 30s at night and maybe 50 during the day. Leaves were turning color and falling off the trees. The sumacs were blood-red. The oaks, maples, and birches were a mixture of yellow, red, purple, green, and brown.

Ezra was scouting for signs of a bobcat or lynx. He had found tracks earlier, and if he could establish their territory, he would get some fine pelts. Beavers were getting scarce, and only a few were left. Muskrats were always near water, along with mink. Now and then, a pine marten was trapped, but they, too, seemed on the decline.

Crouched in some hazelnut bushes, Ezra watched a spike buck eating acorns. He didn't need the venison, so the deer was safe. Easing slowly backward, Ezra stood, turned, and returned to looking for tracks.

Days like this made Ezra sometimes wonder if his pa was still alive. Bertram had always been his own man. He stayed close to nature because he understood it. Yes, it could be harsh and often dangerous, but that was a big part of the lure

of a trapper's life. 'Hope Pa found what he was looking for,'
Ezra thought.

"This letter looks like it was stomped on and dragged
through the mud," Ezra said. The postmark indicated it had
been mailed by the Army postal dept a month ago. Opening
it carefully, Ezra unfolded it and read. "Micah was in his first
big fight," Ezra told Nathan, "in a place called Saint-Mihiel.
It took a few weeks, but the German Army finally gave up
and took off."

"Eban was in a battle in June," Nathan said, "place called
Belleau Wood."

Nodding her head, Rose said, "As long as we keep getting
letters, we know they're alive and well. By the way, Ezra,
Hannah Thorne was in two days ago and asked if you would
ride out to the farm."

"I will do that today," Ezra said.

Conner and Mary Lundtz had two children; the oldest
was Gilbert, and the youngest was Hannah, who was
married to Eban Thorne. While Eban was off fighting the
war, her younger brother, Gilbert, helped run the farm. They
now have a daughter, Esther, just four years old, and a son,
Daniel, two years old.

Ezra had known the Lundtz's since childhood when his
pa worked for Conner. Hannah was like a sister, someone
he cared for. Their properties adjoined along the creek, and
Eban had given Ezra trapping rights on their land. Riding
into the yard, Ezra saw Hannah hanging out a basket of wash.

"I've got a loaf of fresh-baked bread for you," Hannah said, "but first, I want you to find out what has been sneaking into my henhouse and taking my chickens."

Stepping down from the saddle, Ezra smiled. "Let's go take a look." Kneeling by the henhouse, Ezra studied the tracks in the dirt. Rubbing his chin a moment, he stood and said, "It's a fox, maybe a pair because the tracks are a little different size. I'll set some traps later."

Walking back to the house, Ezra asked, "Is Gilbert still considering joining the Navy?"

With a slight grin, Hannah answered, "He hasn't mentioned it lately, and I know he won't leave until Eban returns."

Little Esther walked around the side of the house carrying a small basket with dandelions. Holding the basket up to Ezra, she said, "I got flowers for you."

Kneeling, Ezra lifted out the dandelions and sniffed them. "Thank you, Esther; I'll take them home and put them in water." He gently placed them in a saddlebag and mounted his horse. Hannah had gone in the house and came out with a napkin-wrapped loaf of bread, which also went in the saddlebag. "I'll be back later and set those traps," he said. Tipping his hat, he cantered off.

Early November held a hint of frost as Ezra headed to town. 'I wonder why Micah hasn't written,' Ezra thought. He was at Thorne's Crossroads General Store and Post Office. He did get the weekly newspaper from Burkesville. The headline read BATTLE IN ARGONNE FOREST! The story was about the combined assault against the Germans at the Meuse-Argonne. The Allied forces had kept the German Army in a slow retreat for a month. Heavy losses were taken on both sides.

"There is talk of an Armistice in November," Nathan said. "I sure hope it's true."

"Ezra, do you need any supplies?" asked Rose.

"Two pounds of salt, one pound of sugar, two pounds of ground coffee, and two cans of peaches," Ezra said, "should hold me for a month."

It was late in November. Thanksgiving had come and gone. A light snow had fallen the night before. Ezra was skinning the buck he had shot that morning when Nathan's horse and buggy drove slowly into the yard. Sitting beside him was a man in uniform.

"No," Ezra whispered, "don't let it be." The soldier stepped down from the buggy, holding a leather briefcase.

"Are you Ezra Mulvey?" he asked.

"Is this about my brother, Micah?" asked Ezra.

"Yes, sir, it is. I am Colonel Edward Chadwell, and I bear sad news. Can we go inside and talk?"

"You come too, Nathan," Ezra said, "coffee is hot."

Inside the cabin, Ezra motioned the Colonel to a chair; then he sat while Nathan poured them all coffee. The Colonel took off his hat and set it to one side. "It is my sad duty to inform you that your brother Micah is dead," he said softly. "He died November 1st during the battle of the Meuse-Argonne. A grateful America has awarded him the Silver Star for his heroism in battle."

Standing behind Ezra, Nathan gently laid his hand on

Ezra's shoulder as the Colonel reached into his briefcase and withdrew a letter and a small wooden box. Slowly opening the box, he set it before Ezra. Laying on a blue velvet bed was a shining silver star with a red, white, and blue ribbon attached.

Picking up the letter, the Colonel said, "I would like to read to you the recommendation from his commanding officer, Captain Peterson." Reaching into his jacket pocket, the Colonel took a pair of glasses, put them on, and began reading.

"To the Commanding General of the U.S. Army in France, John J. Pershing. I am recommending Corporal Micah Mulvey for the Silver Star for bravery above and beyond the call of duty." Stopping to clear his throat, the Colonel took a sip of coffee and continued. "On the morning of November 1st, our company was under deadly fire from a German machine gun emplacement. At the risk of his life, Corporal Mulvey, armed with my Colt .45 revolver and a bayonet, managed to circle behind the emplacement and take out the enemy at the cost of his own life." The Colonel stopped reading and slowly lowered the letter.

"I sought out Captain Peterson and found out the whole story," he said.

"Tell me how Micah died," Ezra said softly.

"There were two machine guns in that emplacement, able to cover the entire area where his company was dug in," the Colonel said. "Two crews of three men each were directing a deadly fire when from behind them came Micah. He killed four and wounded two. Out of ammunition, and by now, wounded himself, he drew his bayonet, jumped into the emplacement, and took on the two wounded. He was shot again, this time fatally, but managed to kill the other two Germans. When the company advanced, they found him dead, clutching the bayonet."

Ezra lowered his head. A single tear ran down his cheek and settled on the Silver Star. Nathan, standing behind him, also wept openly. After a long silence, the Colonel said, "Your brother, Corporal Micah Mulvey, was buried with full honors in Arlington Cemetery. A hero's wreath was laid on his grave by the president and General Pershing."

The Colonel rose and, after shaking Ezra's hand, had Nathan drive him back to the store, where a car and driver awaited. For over an hour, Ezra reread the letter and stared at the contents of the wooden box. 'Being alone and being lonely are entirely different,' he thought. 'Being lonely means you miss someone, and my dear brother, you will be missed.'

Two weeks went by. Another snowfall, this one dropping almost two feet of fluffy snow. Ezra had just returned from his trapline. Three muskrats, a mink, and a big pine marten needed to be skinned and the pelts fleshed out.

A lone figure came strolling up the trail from the road. It was Eban Thorne, back from France.

"I'm glad to see you made it back," Ezra said, shaking his friend's hand. "Come inside, and I'll make some coffee."

Sitting at the table, Eban shook his head. "I was sad to hear about Micah. I missed most of the battle; I was in a field hospital. Took some shrapnel in my leg from a German grenade." Setting the coffee pot on the fire, Ezra reached up to the shelf above his bed and took down the small wooden box.

Handing it to Eban, he said, "An Army Colonel came by and gave me this. He told me that crazy brother of mine took on two machine gun crews, six men; killed them all."

Staring at the silver star, Eban said, "Nathan told me they buried him in Arlington Cemetery."

With a sad smile, Ezra said softly, "That's where they bury all the heroes. I am glad you didn't end up there."

Eban smiled. "Hannah would never allow it. You know how stubborn she can be."

"Hannah wouldn't flinch from taking on the Army if it meant having you home." Ezra poured the coffee and sat down.

Taking a sip of the hot brew, Eban said, "Speaking of Hannah, she said to tell you we will be expecting you for Christmas dinner." For a moment, the two men looked at each other, then both smiled.

"I suppose I'll have to shave and probably take a bath," Ezra said.

"Maybe wear a clean shirt, too," Eban added. The cabin filled with laughter, the first happy laughter it had heard in a long time.

CHAPTER FIVE

Mary Lundtz, beloved wife of Conner and mother of Hannah and Gilbert, died within three days from the Spanish flu. The Thorsen family—father, mother, and two young boys—also died. Small towns like Burkesville were hit hard by the deadly virus. No race or gender were immune. And yet, the virus seemed to be selective. It took some and spared others. In 1919, the medical profession had no cure for this flu strain. Doctors could only advise nurses to 'keep the patient as comfortable as you can.'

Mary Lundtz would be missed. She had been active in the church, leading the Ladies Aid Society. As a school board member, she petitioned the governor for new schoolbooks and got them. The community had been a better place because of her.

"I have no interest in becoming a farmer or a logger," Gilbert told Conner. "I am going to enlist in the Navy."

"We just went through a World War," Conner shouted. "What if there is another? You might get killed!"

"That is a chance I am willing to take!" Gilbert shouted back.

Lowering his voice, Conner growled, "If you must go, then you are no longer my son." Without another word,

Gilbert picked up the bag he had packed and stormed out of the house. Conner slowly sank into a kitchen chair. In his anger, he knew he had spoken words he did not mean and could not take back. "God, protect him," he whispered as he hung his head.

Days later, he told Hannah the whole story, leaving nothing out. With her eyes misting over, Hannah gave her father a long hug. "Gilbert is a man now, seeking his path in life. We will pray that God looks after him, and someday he will return. I need to tell Ezra that Gilbert has left. He will worry otherwise."

It took two years for the flu virus to run its course. By 1921, life went on. Change was coming. The tractor was replacing the horse to work the farms. More and more new inventions were flooding the market. New automobiles could be seen daily. Foley Thorne was the blacksmith and spent much of his time redesigning horse-drawn farm equipment for use with tractors.

Nathan and Rose now ran the Crossroads general store. A huge hole had been dug out front, and a large steel tank was installed. A delivery truck arrived every Friday to refill the tank with gasoline. A hand crank pump sat atop the tank, and local farmers now had access to fuel for their new machines.

But one thing stayed the same at the Crossroads: Ezra Mulvey.

His horse no longer shied away or bolted when an auto passed by. Ezra stopped along the side of the dirt road and watched a big LaSalle automobile speed by, leaving a cloud of dust in its wake. Ezra was less than a half-mile from the store and could see the car stop by the gasoline pump. The driver worked the hand pump, filled his tank, and then entered the store.

Ezra stopped at the hitch rail, but before he could dismount, the man came out of the store with a pistol in one hand and a cloth bag in the other. Realizing what happened, Ezra pulled his Colt pistol from the holster.

BANG! BANG!

Both of the LaSalle's rear tires went flat as the robber opened the driver-side door. Throwing his pistol in the air, the robber threw himself flat on the ground, yelling, "Don't shoot me, I give up!" just as Nathan came running from the store holding a shotgun.

"Put the shotgun away, Nathan," Ezra said, "and get some rope. I'll watch him for you."

A farmer and his wife in a flatbed truck stopped. "We are headed into Burkesville," he said. "I'll send the sheriff out for you."

"Tell him to bring a deputy and two spare tires along to drive this LaSalle," Ezra said.

Rose stood on the porch smiling. "Ezra Mulvey. How do you always seem to arrive at just the right moment?"

Ezra put a finger up to his lips and winked. "It's a secret I will take to my grave, Rose."

Nathan had tied the robber's hands and pushed him over to the porch. He handed Rose the cloth sack. "Put this back in the register while I tie his feet."

Dismounting from the horse, Ezra said, "I'll get a can of coffee, tobacco, and the mail and be on my way. Say hello to Luther for me."

It had been overcast all morning. The first drizzle of rain came just before noon. "That's it for today, men," Conner told his barn builders, "looks like this rain will last all afternoon." Then he motioned to Ezra. "I need some help with the new boat I'm building."

"I got nothing planned," Ezra said, "but I could use some lunch first."

"I got ham sandwiches and coffee."

At the kitchen table, Ezra took a bite of his sandwich, washing it down with coffee. "I know you don't cook much. I bet Hannah dropped this off for you."

Conner laughed. "She and Eban stopped by last night, and they always bring me something. She got a letter from Gilbert and read it to me."

"How is he liking the Navy?" Ezra asked.

"The letter said he was in Ireland, and then the ship was on its way to Spain, so I guess he is enjoying himself."

"When he comes back, let me know," Ezra said. "I sure would like to see him again."

"Do you think he will come back?" Conner asked hopefully.

Smiling, Ezra nodded. "If Hannah tells him to, he will."

After lunch, the two men spent the rainy afternoon sanding and shaping the new boat. "The oldest boat at Otter Lake is in rough shape," Conner said. "This new 12-footer will replace that old 10-footer just in time for duck hunting."

"I just bought a new 12-gauge Model '97 Winchester pump shotgun," Ezra said. "I can't wait to try it out."

"You, me, and Eban will be out there on opening day," Conner told him.

Nathan and Rose unpacked and shelved a shipment of men's wool winter shirts. Rose unfolded one and held it up. It was a green and black checkered design with flap pockets.

"I like this one," she said. "I am going to give it to Ezra for helping with the man who tried to rob us."

"I tried to pay him," Nathan said, "but he refused."

"This is not payment; it is a gift, and he *will* accept a gift."

As they worked, Rose asked, "I never see Ezra in church. Does he not believe in God?"

With a sigh, Nathan explained. "He was never taught about God. His parents never owned a Bible or told the boys about religion and churches."

Thinking about it, Rose asked, "Have you ever talked to him about God?"

Nathan knew Rose was not going to drop the subject. "After Micah died, I told Ezra we would have a mass said for him. Ezra answered, 'Don't bother; praying won't bring him back.'

With a sad smile, Rose said, "Well, I pray for him each night and ask God to watch over him."

Nathan took her hand, squeezing it gently. "You, me, Foley, Hannah, and Eban all pray for this man, so I believe his soul is in good hands."

CHAPTER SIX

Foley Thorne broke the news to his family on a fine spring morning in 1922. "Naomi Thompson and I are getting married." Naomi was a young widow whose husband had been killed in the Great War. She had been working as a housekeeper for a local family. Foley had met her at church, and they had been dating for two years. Rose, who had introduced them, had been waiting for this moment.

"Foley Thorne, you are a lucky man," she said. "Naomi has been waiting for you to propose for over a year."

Blushing, Foley said, "I still can't believe that such a wonderful woman wishes to be my wife." Turning to Nathan, he asked, "Will you be my best man?"

"It will be my honor to do so," Nathan said.

"She is coming to the store this morning," Foley told Rose. "She wants you to be her maid of honor."

With a delightful laugh, Rose said, "We will begin to plan the wedding today. Have you chosen a date?"

"Whatever month and day she chooses is fine with me," Foley said.

Ezra rode slowly up to the blacksmith shop. "My horse has a loose shoe," he told Foley. "Left hind hoof."

"I can fix that for you right now, Ezra," he said. "Have you heard I'm getting married?"

"Rose told me yesterday when I picked up my mail," Ezra said. "When is the wedding?"

"Naomi picked Saturday, June 10th," Foley said with a smile. "I expect to see you there."

"I wouldn't miss it," Ezra said.

"Do you think you might ever find a good woman and get married?" Foley asked with a big grin.

"I don't go looking for trouble," Ezra answered, "but it finds me often enough."

Sheriff Luther Godfrey walked up to Ezra's cabin late one afternoon. Ezra was splitting firewood for the cookstove.

He laid down the axe. "Luther, what brings you out this way."

Luther wiped his brow with a big blue handkerchief. "We need to talk, Ezra. As you know, Prohibition is the law of the land."

With a chuckle, Ezra said, "I know just where this is headed. You heard the rumors about my having a still."

Blushing and grinning, Luther nodded his head. "I've been hearing about that still for years. Heard that your pa Bert started it before he left for the Klondike."

"Come on in the cabin and sit," Ezra said. "Hannah left me some fresh buttermilk this morning. We will share it, and I will tell you about the still."

They went inside, and the sheriff took a chair. A half-gallon stoneware jug was sitting in a pan of cold water. Ezra popped the cork and poured them each a glass. Luther took a drink, wiped his chin, and said, "Tastes mighty good on a hot day."

Sitting, Ezra said, "There never has been a still, Luther. Pa had no idea how to make one, and I don't either."

With a slight frown, Luther said, "Well, how on earth did that rumor ever get started?"

With a grin, Ezra held up the jug of buttermilk. "It started with this jug. Whenever Hannah churns butter, she fills this jug and has Eban leave it in the creek to keep it cold. When the buttermilk is gone, I put it back in the creek in another spot nearby to let them know."

Scratching his head, Luther asked, "But how did the moonshine rumor start?"

"Probably the Hatch boys," Ezra answered. "They must have seen the jug in the creek and thought it was liquor. They are always sneaking around other people's property."

"Why didn't they take the jug?"

"Because I would know who took it. The Hatch's are lazy thieves, but neither want to get shot."

Luther's eyes grew wide. "Would you shoot them, Ezra?"

"Wouldn't kill one, just hurt them a little. Small price to pay for stealing a man's buttermilk."

Ezra squatted on the crest of a low hill, watching two black bear cubs playing below. They were off to his right, chasing each other up and down a maple tree. 'Might make a fine pelt in about three years,' he thought.

Tied well back in the trees, his horse began grunting and snorting. Ezra turned his head to the left and caught the foul odor of bear. Purely by instinct, he threw his body forward and to the left, away from the cubs. His actions were quick but not quick enough. The mother bear had crept up behind him without a sound. With a brutal swipe of her big paw, she caught Ezra across the back, her long claws tearing through his shirt and into his flesh.

As he rolled downward, Ezra managed to pull his Colt from the holster and get off two quick shots into the air, hoping to scare the bear. It worked. The cubs, startled by the shots, ran to their mother, who turned and ran also. Ezra lay in the grass and leaves, glad to be alive.

As he crawled up the hill, the movements sent shock waves through his body. He broke into a sweat as he slowly mounted the horse. 'If I can make it to the store, Rose can patch me up,' he thought.

The pain was like nothing he had felt before. It throbbed and burned from his neck to his waist. Finally, he reached the road. He had more than a mile to go and hoped to make it before passing out.

Nathan was sweeping off the porch when he saw the horse with Ezra bent over the saddle horn. Throwing down the broom, he ran to the horse and grabbed the bridle, leading it to the hitching rail.

"Rose, come quick!" he yelled. Nathan caught Ezra as he was sliding from the saddle.

Rose raced through the open door. "Oh my God!" she choked. "His back is torn to shreds!"

"Rose. Get the truck. We need to take him to the Burkesville hospital."

Nathan eased a now unconscious Ezra onto the seat of

the vehicle and then turned toward his wife. "Unsaddle the horse and turn it into the stock pen," he said. "I'll be back when I can."

Reaching the hospital, Nathan jumped out of the truck and yanked open the hospital's front door. "I need a gurney and a doctor right now!"

A moment later, a nurse appeared, pushing a gurney. She was middle-aged, stout, with short brown hair.

"Help me load him on the gurney," she said. "The doctor will be with us in a minute." Together, Nathan and the nurse lifted Ezra from the truck. Taking a look at the wounds, she said, "Lay him face down."

As they wheeled Ezra through the door, the doctor hurried to them.

"What happened?" he asked as they rolled the gurney into an examination room.

"He came to about halfway to town," Nathan said, "all he said was 'black bear,' then he passed out again."

"Cut the shirt off so I can see the extent of the wound," the doctor instructed. Turning to Nathan, he said, "I see bright red blood, which tells me no arteries are open. It's a serious wound but not life-threatening. Do you know him?"

Nathan let out a big sigh of relief. "He's my neighbor and best friend, Ezra Mulvey."

The nurse returned with the scissors and started cutting the shirt off.

"First, we have to clean the wound completely, then I get to play seamstress for a few hours. If he regains consciousness, we will administer chloroform, but not until." Laying his hand on Nathan's shoulder, the doctor told him, "Give the lady at the front desk all the information you can, then go home. You can check on him tomorrow morning."

Ezra awoke just before midnight. Lying on his stomach, he recalled some things from hours before. He remembered being in Nathan's truck and, later, the strange smell of alcohol mixed with blood and a sweet-smelling cloth pressed over his nose and mouth. He tried to move and found his legs and arms strapped down. The agonizing pain from the attack had become a low, steady ache across his entire back. Gratefully, he settled back to sleep.

He awoke again at 7 am. He was still on his stomach but no longer strapped down. The nurse gently removed the dressing from his back.

"Good morning, Mr. Mulvey. How are you feeling?"

"I need water," Ezra croaked.

"As soon as the doctor examines you, I will get you some water," she replied.

The doctor entered, saying, "As soon as I admire my needlework, I will have the nurse get you some breakfast and coffee. I'm Doctor Nelson," he said as he gently poked and prodded Ezra's back. "Tell me how you came by this bizarre wound."

"Water first," Ezra said.

Nodding to the nurse, the doctor said, "Just a few sips."

His dry throat now eased, Ezra related his story. "I got between a she-bear and her cubs. How bad did she get me?"

"You have four claw wounds extending from your left shoulder to your right hip. The two center wounds are the deepest. Luckily, no major arteries opened, and there was no damage to your spine. It could have been much worse. As it is, there is still the possibility of infection, so we will have to keep you here for a few days until I feel it is safe for you to go home. Do you feel you can keep food down?"

"I am hungry," Ezra said.

"Put a clean dressing on and get him some food," the doctor said. "He may sit up with a pillow behind him to eat and then on his side to rest."

Every Thorne family member paid a visit, as did Sheriff Godfrey and Conner Lundtz. Hannah Thorne bought him a shirt. "It's soft cotton, so it won't irritate your stitches," she said.

Nathan showed up with a pair of pants. "Yours are so bloody they are stiff as a board," he said.

"Where is my revolver?" Ezra asked.

"I took it home with me," Nathan said. "The nurses didn't want it here."

Foley and his new wife, Naomi, snuck in some homemade cookies.

"Beats the hell out of flowers," said Ezra.

When Luther Godfrey visited, he wanted to know "how is the food here?"

"Hardly enough for a man to live on, and it has no taste. Salt don't even help," Ezra told him.

After three days, the doctor released Ezra. "No physical activity for a week," the doctor ordered. "We have a new county nurse. Her name is Regina Forrest. I will have her stop by and change your bandage in two days."

"Don't need no nurse," Ezra said.

"In that case," the doctor said with a smile, "we'll keep you here two more days."

Ezra and the doctor stared at each other for a very long moment, then Ezra said, "Tell her I'll be waiting."

As Ezra climbed into Nathan's truck wearing his cotton shirt and clean pants, Nathan handed him his Colt revolver with the belt and holster. Nodding his thanks, Ezra said, "Some nurse is coming by to check my bandage in a few days."

"You do what she tells you," Nathan said, "and you might live to kill that old bear."

The two friends began laughing.

CHAPTER SEVEN

Sitting on the bench outside, Ezra watched the woman walking up the trail to his cabin. She was tall, with a trim figure, about 5 foot 9 inches, maybe 25 years old, with dark blonde hair tied back with a ribbon. She wore a tan shirt and loose denim trousers. She walked with easy grace, like she was just out for a stroll. In her left hand, she carried a doctor's bag.

As she neared, she smiled and held out her hand. "Good morning, Mr. Mulvey; I'm the county nurse, Regina Forrest."

Ezra shook her hand, "Doc Nelson said you would be stopping by. Want some coffee?"

"I would like that, but first, let me look at your back." With practiced hands, Regina undid the bandage and lightly probed Ezra's stitches. "All the stitches are still in place, and there is no sign of infection," she told him. "I'm going to put some ointment on and a clean bandage."

As she worked, Regina asked, "Have you had any unusual pain or loss of feeling in your back?"

"Nothing unusual," Ezra said. "When can the stitches come out?"

"If all goes well," she replied while applying a fresh

bandage, "I can remove them in a week. Now, how about that coffee?"

Sitting at the kitchen table, Ezra asked, "Why did you become a nurse?"

"Because I didn't want to be a doctor," Regina said.

With a puzzled frown, Ezra said, "Not sure I understand."

With a smile, Regina said, "I volunteered to help the nurses in Milwaukee during the war. I liked helping people, so I later went to nursing school. I hate the thought of cutting people open; I just want to help them get well."

"Is Milwaukee your hometown?" Ezra asked.

"Yes, it is. But after being out in the country, I could never live in a big city again. Well, I have more people to see, so I must be on my way."

As promised, a week later, the nurse was back. On the bench outside the cabin, Regina had laid a white towel. On the towel were a small bottle of alcohol, tweezers, small scissors, and several small white pads. Ezra had carried a chair outside and now straddled it, his arms resting on the back.

"Mr. Mulvey, I am going to hold the stitches with the tweezers, cut them, and pull them out."

Turning his head to look back at Regina, he said, "My friends call me Ezra."

"Alright, Ezra. Mine call me Gina," she replied. When the first stitch came out, one bright red spot of blood appeared. With an alcohol-soaked pad, Gina pressed softly on the spot and waited a moment. Taking the cloth away, the red spot was gone. In less than an hour, all the stitches were out.

"I can give you a clean bill of health," Gina said. "Now,

how about some coffee?" Back in the cabin, Gina took a sip of hot coffee. "What do you do when you're not fighting with bears?"

"In the summer, I help build barns," Ezra told her, "and in the winter, I trap. I was scouting out new territory when that mother bear snuck up behind me." Looking closer, Ezra noticed Gina's eyes. One was brown, and one was blue.

"You are staring at my eyes," Gina said with a slight smile.

With a slight grin, Ezra said, "Yes, and I like what I see."

Gina blushed and replied, "I will take that as a compliment."

Finishing her coffee, Gina stood and said, "I will be back to check on you next week."

Ezra watched as she walked down the trail. Without turning around, she lifted her arm and waved goodbye.

The flatbed truck sat nose-down in the ditch. The passenger side door was open, and a man lay dead, holding a revolver. Sheriff Luther Godfrey, a deputy, and Ezra exited the sheriff's car and approached the truck.

"A farmer on his way into town saw this about dawn," the deputy said.

"Don't get too close," Ezra cautioned. "I want to look the ground over for tracks." Stepping carefully around to the driver's side, Ezra looked inside. "Got a dead driver," he said, "can see at least two bullet holes." Then Ezra moved around to the front of the truck and knelt, slowly rolling the dead man over. Standing, he carefully looked the ground over, slowly shaking his head.

Looking in the bed of the truck, Ezra touched a wet

spot and sniffed. "They were hauling whiskey. Whoever shot them took it."

The sheriff was looking at the dead passenger. "I don't recognize this one," he said, "probably not local." Moving around to the driver's side, he opened the door. The driver lay over the steering wheel, his arms hanging straight down, his head turned toward the sheriff. "Don't know this one either."

Ezra was walking away from the front of the truck and stopped. "Luther. Got a blood trail here," he called, "not dried yet, maybe a couple of hours old."

"Think you can find him?" asked Luther.

"Bleeding or not, I'll find him," Ezra said.

"I'm going back to Burkesville for a tow truck and an ambulance," Luther said. "Do you need my Winchester?"

"No," Ezra said, patting his holster. "It would just get in the way. When you return, honk your horn so I know it's you."

Ezra found the wounded man in the woods about a mile from the truck. He was sitting against a tree, head back and eyes closed. Next to him lay a Model 1911 Colt, the slide locked back, empty. Walking up slowly, Ezra gently kicked the man's outstretched right foot. Startled, the man looked up, saw Ezra standing over him, and grabbed for his gun. "Don't bother," Ezra told him. "It's empty."

Looking closely, Ezra saw two wounds, one in the upper left arm and the other in the left thigh.

"I think I'm dying," the man whispered.

"No, you'll live," Ezra said. "What's your name?"

"George Doemel," he said. "My pal left me for dead and took off with the booze."

"Not your pal anymore, I'll bet," Ezra said, smiling.

"If I see him again, I'll kill him," George snarled.

A distant honk filtered through the trees, along with the soft whine of an ambulance. Ezra pulled a large, red-checked handkerchief from his pocket and tied it tightly around the wounded leg. "I'm going to carry you out of here," he said. "It's going to hurt, but I'll take it as easy as I can." Ezra picked up the empty Colt and stuck it in his pocket. Holding the man's good arm and leg, he picked him up in a fireman's carry and started walking.

The sheriff's car, a tow truck, and an ambulance were there when Ezra stepped out of the woods. George had passed out from the pain a while back and was just dead weight.

"Here comes Ezra," a deputy shouted. In addition to Sheriff Godfrey and the deputy, the tow truck driver, the ambulance driver, and Regina Forrest waited along the side of the road.

"He's alive," Ezra said. "Let's get him in the ambulance." With the sheriff and deputy helping, George was soon lying on the gurney with Regina cutting away his clothes to get at his wounds. Reaching into his pocket, Ezra handed Luther the Colt pistol.

"Good thinking, bringing the nurse along," Ezra grinned.

"When she heard you were tracking a wounded man, she insisted on coming along," Luther said. "Did you find out anything about him?"

"His name is George Doemel, and his pal left him for dead," Ezra said. "They were after the whiskey, don't know how much."

Regina stepped down from the ambulance. "That man

owes you his life, Ezra. If you hadn't found him, he would have died out in those woods."

"Just glad I could help, Gina," Ezra said with a smile.

Regina got back in the ambulance, and they drove away. Luther Godfrey had a smile playing at the corner of his mouth. "Fine-looking woman, that new nurse," he said. "I take it you two know each other."

"She took the stitches out of my back," Ezra said, "didn't hurt a bit."

"I didn't see a ring," Luther said. "She must be single."

Ezra looked the sheriff in the eye. "Don't know because I didn't ask. She does like my coffee, though."

"King me," Rufus Dawes said with a grin.

With a grunt, Nathan topped the black checker with another. "Might get some frost tonight," he said as he slid his red checker across the board.

"Don't think so," Rufus said, "too early."

The small bell above the door tinkled as Ezra entered the store, followed by Regina Forrest.

"Who's winning?" Ezra asked.

"Me, as usual!" Rufus said. "Your back all healed up, Ezra?"

"Healed just fine, left a wicked scar to show." Then Ezra motioned toward Regina. "Allow me to introduce Miss Regina Forrest, the county nurse."

As Rufus stood, Regina noticed the wooden leg just below the man's left knee.

"You would be Rufus Dawes," she said, holding out her hand.

As Rufus shook her hand, he said, "Lost the leg years ago in a log jam at Rocky Falls by Merrill."

"If it ever bothers you, let someone know, and I will stop by," said Regina.

"I want to show Gina some of the countryside," Ezra told Nathan, "if we can borrow a horse and saddle."

Just then, Rose walked in from the post office, and a smile lit up her pretty face. "Hello, Miss Forrest," she said. "I'm Rose Thorne, Nathan's wife. It is my pleasure to meet you."

As the two women shook hands, Regina said, "Please call me Gina. Ezra has offered to take me on a tour of his domain if I can borrow a horse."

"Take that pinto mare in the stock pen," Rose told her. "She rides easy as a rocking chair."

After Ezra and Regina left the store, Rose stood smiling, tapping her finger against her chin.

"You stop that right now!" Nathan said.

"Stop what?" Rose smiled with a completely innocent look.

"I know you all too well, Rose Thorne," Nathan said, pointing a finger at her. "In that Irish mind of yours, you have already got them two married. Maybe they are just friends."

Rose left the room with an exasperated sigh, muttering something about men being dense.

CHAPTER EIGHT

"It is just beautiful," Regina sighed. They sat their horses atop a small hill overlooking a valley of wildflowers. A creek running through added a ribbon of sparkling blue, and the birches surrounding it were like a picture frame.

"I never imagined such a place existed," Regina said softly. Turning in her saddle to look at Ezra, she grinned and asked, "Do you bring all your female friends here?"

Smiling shyly, Ezra answered, "Never brought anyone else here. I thought you might like it."

Regina gave him a long look, blushed slightly, then smiled. "I will think of this place whenever I am sad, and it will bring me peace," she said softly.

From a distance, they watched a fox with two kits playing. Later, Ezra showed her a large nest high in an old oak tree. "A pair of eagles have raised several young up there," Ezra said. "When the young are full grown, they find mates and build their own nest. Eagles are like Canada geese; they mate for life." It was an afternoon Regina would remember long after the ride was over.

As the horses walked side by side, Ezra said, "Tell me about your family." Regina was quiet for a moment as if deciding whether or not to reply. Then she began.

"My father died from a massive stroke when I was ten years old. He was a bank auditor for several large banks in Milwaukee. One day, he went to work and never came home." She paused, sighed, and continued. "He had insurance, so Mother and I had no worries. Needing to keep busy, Mother took a position at the library, only a block from the school where I was enrolled."

Regina smiled, remembering the past. "Mother would walk me to school and back home every weekday. Some weekends, we would take the train to Racine and visit with Mother's only sister, my Aunt Helen." Regina stopped her horse, and so did Ezra, with a tear sliding down her cheek. "That damned flu came and took my mother and my aunt. Why I was spared, I will never know."

Regina was openly crying now. Ezra swung down from his horse and helped Regina dismount. "I hate crying," she said softly, "it serves no purpose."

Ezra took a red handkerchief from his pocket and wiped Regina's cheeks. "Without tears, there would be little need for handkerchiefs."

With a little laugh, Regina took the handkerchief and dabbed at her eyes. Looking up at Ezra, she said, "Now that we are telling our life stories, tell me yours."

"We are almost back to the cabin," Ezra said. "I will tell you as we ride."

Ezra and Regina returned to the store as the sun met the horizon. "Can we do this again?" Regina asked.

"Yes," Ezra said, "if you promise not to cry again." They both started laughing and then, with an unspoken agreement, they hugged. Regina got in her auto and drove away. Rose, watching from the store window, came out on the porch.

"Did you have a pleasant ride?" she asked.

"Probably the best ride I have had in years," Ezra said with a smile.

"It seems the new nurse likes your company," Rose said.

"I want to buy this pinto horse and the saddle," Ezra said with a grin, "then Gina and I can ride whenever we like." Rose giggled, clapped her hands, and ran into the store to tell Nathan.

Percy Jones slipped out of the barn he had been sleeping in around midnight. Three other men were sleeping there, and he didn't want to wake them. Percy was part of a work detail offered by the local jail to area farmers. Due to the war and the dreaded flu epidemic, there was a distinct shortage of men to labor on the farms. A deal had been worked out with the local authorities to allow prisoners, who were in custody for minor offenses, the opportunity to do farm work. They were paid nothing but fed well.

Percy had been caught burglarizing a hardware store. Police had captured him on his way into the store, so he hadn't had time to steal anything. He was charged with breaking and entering. For three months, he was a model prisoner and welcomed the chance to be anywhere but in jail. After a week on the farm, Percy made his move.

With only a sliver of moon showing, Percy set out across the field. They had been shocking corn stalks that day, and in the darkness, he stumbled into two shocks. His goal was the woods beyond the cornfield, then across the creek and onto the railroad tracks. There, he hoped to ride an empty boxcar to freedom.

The gray light of dawn was beginning to push back the shadows of night as Sheriff Luther Godfrey knocked on Ezra Mulvey's door.

"Come on in and sit down," Ezra said, "coffee is ready."

Ezra finished shaving and splashed cold water on his face. "Pour us both a cup, then tell me why you are out this early," Ezra called.

When Eza entered the room, Luther donned a wicked little grin. "Why are you shaving on a Monday morning? Expecting company?"

"None of your damned business," Ezra answered. "Just tell me what you want."

Luther sipped his coffee. "Jonas Zimmerman got me out of bed to tell me one of my prisoners working on his farm took off last night. I was hoping you could track him down for me."

"Tell me about him?" Ezra asked.

"His name is Percy Jones. He is a skinny runt, 25 years old, about 5 foot 6 inches tall, wearing overalls and a green shirt."

"You go tell Jonas I will be there in about an hour," Ezra told him.

"Will do." Luther drained his mug. Then, looking around, he said, "This place is so clean, I could eat off the floor."

"Just get in your car and go," Ezra growled, giving Luther a friendly shove toward the door. "I'll meet you at the farm."

Jonas and his three remaining helpers let the cows out

after milking. Sheriff Godfrey stood beside his car when Ezra rode into the yard. "He must have left about midnight," Jonas said, "don't miss him; he wasn't much of a worker."

Ezra looked across the cornfield. "Appears he knocked down two corn shocks on his way to the woods, probably headed for the train tracks."

"He's got a good 6-hour head start," Luther said. "Can you find him before he gets there?" Leaning over his saddle horn and grinning, Ezra said, "There is a county road running alongside the tracks. You drive out there, and I will bring him to you."

'This could be the easiest tracking I've ever done,' thought Ezra. Percy did not try to hide his route. He stumbled often on the uneven ground, broke any brush that got in his way, almost lost one of his shoes in the mud along the creek, and left a small torn piece of overalls on a broken-down barbwire fence. Coming out to a small open meadow, Ezra could hardly believe what he saw and just stopped and stared.

Percy was hopping up and down, waving his arms and screaming!

"Damned fool walked right into a ground-wasp nest," Ezra chuckled softly. Then, Percy took off running, stumbled over an anthill, and fell. Riding wide around the wasp nest, Ezra brought his horse to a halt just a few feet from Percy.

Looking up at Ezra, the man shouted, "Who the hell are you!"

Smiling, Ezra said, "Get on your feet and start walking. We have about a mile to go to the train track."

With snot running from his nose and tears in his eyes,

Percy shouted, "You go to hell!" Ezra slowly pulled his Colt from the holster and fired a shot at Percy's feet.

BANG!

Percy jumped up, yelling, "Don't shoot me, don't shoot me!"

"Just start walking," Ezra told him. With a resigned sigh, Percy began walking.

Sheriff Godfrey sat in his car, watching the road in both directions. About a quarter mile away, he saw a man stumble through the tall grass and onto the road, followed by a man on a horse. He started his car and drove up to them.

Getting out, Luther said, "What took you so long?"

"Percy stopped to play with some wasps," Ezra said. "He got stung pretty good." The man had several red welts on his face and hands.

"This man tried to shoot me!" Percy protested.

"That's nonsense," Luther said. "If he had, you would be dead." Luther handcuffed Percy and placed him in the backseat of his patrol car. Turning to Ezra, he asked, "How much does the county owe you for this?"

"I'll send them a bill someday," Ezra said as he rode away. Slowly shaking his head, Luther knew there would never be a bill.

CHAPTER NINE

"Nathan, come look at this," Rose yelled. She was in the storeroom, sweeping the floor, when she noticed corn was slowly leaking out of a small hole in a ten-pound bag of seed corn. Looking closer, she could see the edges of the hole were ragged. Something had chewed a hole in the bag, which seemed fairly recent.

Nathan walked into the storeroom as Rose poked a finger into the hole. Nathan turned the bag on its side and said, "I'll get another bag; just pick up the corn off the floor." With Rose's help, the seed corn was soon safe in a new bag.

"Looks like we have a hungry rat," Nathan said. "I'll set out some traps tonight, and by tomorrow morning, we should have our culprit."

After setting two big rat traps, Nathan wondered 'How did the rat get in?' Moving aside several barrels and wooden boxes, he found a board with a weathered knot in one corner of the storeroom that had come loose a few inches above the floor. The knot had been pushed in and was lying on the floor. 'Seems like a mighty small hole for a rat,' thought Nathan.

Nailing a foot-square piece of board over the hole, Nathan muttered, "If he is out, he will stay out, and if he is in, I will catch him."

The sun was barely up the next morning when Nathan started the coffee brewing in the kitchen and went to the storeroom. The sun winked through the high window enough for Nathan to see an animal in one of the traps, not caught by the neck but by a front leg. The animal bared its teeth and awkwardly lunged at Nathan. Backing up quickly, he slammed the door and stood there shaking his head.

'Gotta talk to Ezra about this,' he thought. Walking back to the kitchen, he met Rose.

"Did we catch a rat?" she asked.

"We caught . . . something," Nathan said, "but it's not a rat. Maybe Ezra will know what it is."

"You caught a young mink." Ezra had stopped to check his mail, and Nathan explained the incident with the seed corn and the knothole. "Mink like living around water," he explained, "but dry land suits them too. Mink have a nose like a bloodhound; this one probably smelled that corn and found a way in. I'll take it with me and dress it out for you."

"What can I do with it?" Nathan asked.

"Might make a nice collar for Rose's winter coat," Ezra said with a grin.

One fall morning, Ezra rode into the front yard of Eban and Hannah Thorne's farm. A pair of matched Belgian workhorses were hitched to a wagon by the big oak tree. Eban came out of the front door, holding a cup of coffee.

"Ready to make some firewood?" he asked.

"First coffee, then firewood," Ezra answered.

In the kitchen, Hannah poured Ezra a cup. "I know it's a

little early to ask," she said, "but are you having Thanksgiving with Regina?"

With a shy smile, Ezra said, "It's almost like you can read my mind, Hannah. I was going to ask if you minded Gina having Thanksgiving here with us."

Hannah's smile lit up the kitchen. "Having another woman in the kitchen would make my day," she said. "No need to bring any food; all we need is right here."

The woodlot rang with the sound of axes and saws. The trees cut down last year were now dried and ready to be made into winter fuel. The trees were limbed off, cut into lengths, and loaded on the wagon. Long, thick branches were trimmed and added to the growing pile – primarily hardwoods but a few pines for hot kitchen fires.

When the sun was at its peak, the men stopped for a lunch of sandwiches and lukewarm coffee from a thermos.

"You seem to get along pretty well with Regina," Eban said as they ate.

Thinking a moment, as if deciding on the right answer, Ezra said, "We enjoy each other's company. In some ways, we are a lot alike; both of us have lost family."

Eban lit his pipe. "Sometimes, the world unfolds in ways we can never understand. All we can do is go with our heart and hope for the best."

Ezra gave his friend a long look, then grinned. "Hannah's been reading the Bible to you again, hasn't she?" Both men started laughing! It floated through the woodlot like a happy song.

Hannah Thorne had two passions in her life. Her relationship with God began as a child and sustained her through the hard times growing up. Her husband and children were loved with that same passion. Her eldest child, Esther, was now 7, Daniel was 5, Jacob was 2, and the youngest, Noah, was just out of diapers and usually underfoot.

The kitchen was Hannah's domain. The farm and the garden provided most of what the family needed, and wild game completed the family's needs. Grouse, rabbits, ducks, geese, and venison were often a staple of the meals served. This year, Thanksgiving dinner would be ducks, provided by her father, Conner, who would be joining them for the feast.

Thanksgiving morning dawned clear and cold. As Hannah had requested, Ezra and Regina arrived at the Thorne farm at 8 am.

"Hang your coats in the mudroom and sit for coffee," Hannah said.

Regina wore a red and white gingham dress and low-heeled shoes. Blushing a little, she told Hannah, "I haven't worn a dress in so long it feels like I am a different person."

Smiling, Hannah replied, "You look lovely, Gina. We are so glad you came." Then, turning to Ezra, she said, "And who is this gentleman wearing a white shirt and new vest?"

Grinning, Ezra said, "A bath, a shave, and some new clothes, but still the same old me."

"Take your coffee into the parlor with Eban while us ladies prepare a meal," Hannah told him.

Blushing slightly, Regina said, "I'm afraid I won't be much help, Hannah. I've never learned to cook. We always had a housekeeper who did the shopping and cooking. I can fry an egg and make toast, but that is the extent of my cooking."

Hannah took both of Regina's hands in hers. "God has given each of us a role in life. Eban is a farmer and a wonderful husband and father. I am a farmer's wife and a mother. You are a nurse who cares for the sick and injured, but you are also an intelligent woman, and today, while Esther is peeling potatoes, you will learn to make biscuits!"

Taking down a large stoneware bowl from a shelf, Hannah said, "You start with 3 cups of flour, a pinch of baking powder, and a dab of water. Mix it thoroughly until you have dough. When it is ready, let me know."

In the parlor, the flames danced behind the isinglass window of the big woodstove. Daniel and Jacob lay belly-down on the big rug, playing checkers as Noah watched. The men talked of logging, farming, hunting, fishing, and trapping. From the kitchen came the sounds of women talking and laughing. Ezra was feeling new emotions and enjoying them. The time spent with Regina had given him a new insight into caring for a woman. He allowed himself to wonder if this could be love. It was all so new to him and yet so natural. His thoughts were interrupted when Conner arrived.

Carrying a cup of coffee, Conner joined the men in the parlor. "Grandpa!" the boys shouted and ran to hug him.

Sitting down, Conner said, "Ezra, I am happy to see you invited Regina along; she seems to be enjoying herself in the kitchen."

"I thought you would be on your way to the Brule River logging camp," Ezra said.

"I will be leaving on the train tomorrow morning,"

Conner replied. "My trunk is packed and waiting at the station."

"I am surprised we haven't had a decent snowfall yet," Eban said.

"I'll be setting out my trapline tomorrow morning," Ezra said. "I found signs of a pair of bobcats last week."

Their talk was interrupted by Esther calling, "Dinner is ready!"

Along with the roast duck were mashed potatoes, gravy, green beans (canned that summer), a tart cranberry sauce, biscuits, apple cider, and coffee. As the elder, Conner said grace, blessing the food and all at the table.

"Pass the biscuits again, please," Eban asked.

"Gina made the biscuits," Hannah told everyone, "and with a few more lessons, will probably out-cook me."

Laughing and blushing, Gina said, "No one will ever out-cook you, Hannah. This duck is the best I have ever eaten." And it was. Golden brown outside, tender and juicy inside.

"You can thank my mother, Mary, who taught me all I know in the kitchen." For dessert, pumpkin and apple pies were served. They all lingered over the meal, not wanting to break the spell cast by family and friends, celebrating.

Finally, after the table was cleared, the dishes were done, and parcels of wrapped leftovers were handed out, Conner said goodbye. "I will see you all in the spring when we send the logs downriver," he promised.

Gina hugged Esther and Hannah, saying, "This was the most wonderful Thanksgiving I have ever had, thank you."

"When you come for Christmas, I will have you make a pie," Hannah said with a smile.

Turning to Ezra, Gina said, "We will be here for Christmas, won't we?"

Ezra placed his arm around her shoulders. "We will be here right after church service."

Hannah gasped, putting her hand to her mouth. Ezra grinned and said, "That ought to shake up the whole county."

Driving back to Ezra's cabin, Gina told Ezra, "It was the first time I had ever tried to cook anything. Hannah talked me through it, but I did everything! I kneaded and rolled with the rolling pin, layered the dough, made the biscuits, and put them in the oven. Did everyone really like them?"

Ezra was grinning. "You made twelve biscuits, and they were all eaten except one, which I have in the leftovers Hannah sent with us. They were delicious!"

When they reached the cabin, Ezra asked, "Would you like some coffee?"

Laying her hand on his cheek, Gina said softly, "I would, but I am going to say no. If you get me in your cabin, I won't want to leave, and I have a very busy day tomorrow. Do you understand?"

Taking her flushed face in his hands, Ezra said in a hushed voice, "I am going to kiss you goodnight and let you go for now."

As their lips met, Gina felt the gentleness of this man who seemed so rough on the outside. Her arms went around him as she pressed against him. Then, they parted, both with the understanding that an unspoken promise had passed between them. They both knew they were in love.

CHAPTER TEN

It was a week before Christmas, and the general store was a busy place with purchases of flour, sugar, nutmeg, cinnamon, baking powder, and all the secret spices the women needed for that special treat for the holidays. Nathan and Rose opened the doors early and stayed late to help fill the orders. Gifts like mittens, a wool scarf, lined leather gloves, long underwear, and socks were often included.

Ezra was out of his element, looking for a gift for Gina. Rose watched him for a few moments, then asked, "Do you know what you are looking for?"

Scratching his chin, Ezra said, "I need to find a special gift for Gina, but I am not sure what."

Thinking a moment, Rose said, "Gina spends a lot of time outdoors in the winter. I have something that might make her very happy." From a lower shelf, Rose took out a box and opened it. Inside were a pair of women's lined leather boots. They were dark brown, sturdy, but flexible, with low heels and laces.

"If you get a size or two larger than she usually wears, she can wear wool socks in them, and I will give you a tin of mink oil to waterproof them," Rose said.

Thinking a moment, Ezra grinned and said, "I'll take them with two pairs of socks."

Giggling, Rose told him, "I will Christmas wrap them for you tonight, and you can pick them up tomorrow."

Shyly, Ezra said, "This is the first time I have bought her a gift; I hope she will like it."

Rose laid her hand on Ezra's arm. "If you gave her a winter-killed cabbage, she would love it because it came from you."

Abel Schwanke sat in the kitchen of his farmhouse with his foot propped up on a three-legged stool with a small bag of ice draped over it. His ankle was swollen as big as a turnip and ached. Abel was 35 years old, stout but in good health.

"You sit right there," his wife, Gladys, said. "The boys can handle the chores for a few days."

Abel ran a small farm, milking only ten cows. His two sons, Louis, age 12, and John, now 14, could handle the milking and feeding; it was not being able to help that had Abel frustrated. He should be out hunting. He was counting on some venison for Christmas dinner. The boys were still in school, and Gladys was not a hunter.

"Have some coffee," his wife said, handing him a steaming mug. The dog started barking out in the yard, and then a knock came at the door.

"Come in, Ezra," she said as she opened the door. "I just made a fresh pot of coffee."

Entering, Ezra looked at Abel's ankle. "I heard one of your cows kicked you, but good."

Wincing as he leaned forward to shake Ezra's hand, Abel said, "Caught me right on the bone, she did. The county nurse was by and said to stay off it for a week."

"Good advice. Give it time to heal." Sipping his coffee, Ezra asked, "Got your deer yet?"

"Hell no," Abel grimaced, "and it looks like I won't have any venison this year."

Grinning, Ezra said, "Well, it just so happens I have a fat 4-pointer on the back of my saddle right now. Thought me and your boys could skin it out and quarter it for you." Abel's mouth dropped open, snapped shut, and opened again.

"Why are you doing this, Ezra?" Abel asked.

Smiling, Ezra said, "Everyone knows you like venison roast for Christmas dinner. Now, I can't spend all night chatting with you when I have work to do."

Gladys stepped forward, taking one of Ezra's hands in hers. "Hang the buck in the machine shed; there's a rope and pulley already there. And God bless you, Ezra Mulvey."

A light snow began falling on Christmas Eve. There was already a foot of snow on the ground from two days before. The temperature hovered between 15 and 20 degrees. By Christmas morning, the world had become a winter wonderland of snow-covered trees, bushes, and buildings. Farm chores were mixed with snowball throwing and cries of 'quit playing and start milking.'

Families dressed in their warmest clothing made their way to the Crossroads church. The sun shining through the stained-glass windows cast its light on the manger scene to the right of the alter. Candles burned brightly everywhere, adding a flickering glow to the polished pews. People filled the seats, whispering 'Merry Christmas' to their neighbors.

Eban and Hannah entered with their children, taking their usual pew. The last couple to enter sent a hushed gasp through the congregation. Ezra Mulvey escorted Regina Forrest to the pew in front of the Thorne family. The vestibule doors were closed, and the service began. There was a tear in the corner of Hannah's eye as she raised her lovely face to the heavens and whispered a silent 'Thank you' to her Lord.

Back at the Thorne farm, Hannah's venison roast, which was in the oven to slow roast during church, filled the kitchen with a mouth-watering aroma. On the counter sat two pies: an apple and a strawberry-rhubarb.

"Eban, would you please light the candles on the tree?" Hannah asked. The banked fire in the parlor stove was replenished with more wood. In the kitchen, Hannah, Esther, and Gina made coffee, poured out the apple cider, and loaded a tray with cookies and fruitcake.

When all were settled, Eban said, "Last year, Esther handed out the gifts; this year, Daniel will do so." Hannah had been busy knitting all year, and everyone got just what they needed: mittens, scarves, caps, and even a sweater-vest for Eban.

Gina was overjoyed with her boots. "My feet always get cold in my old leather boots, even with wool socks," she said. "These boots are just what I needed. Thank you, Ezra."

Hannah admired her new flannel nightgown. "I certainly hinted often enough, didn't I, Eban?" she said with a smile.

Ezra received a fur-lined cap with earmuffs. "Rose helped me pick it out," Gina said.

"My old stocking cap is now retired," Ezra said.

For Eban, a large can of apple-blend pipe tobacco – his favorite.

Esther and Daniel each got a new winter coat. "They are growing up so quickly," Hannah said. "I am sure they will be tall like their father."

The Christmas dinner was the perfect finish to a wonderful day: tender and juicy venison roast, mashed potatoes, gravy, peas and carrots, hot dinner rolls from the oven, coffee and apple cider, and pie for dessert. The talk ranged from past Christmases to what the future might hold.

"I decided to add a few more cows to the herd this spring," Eban said, "and I planted winter wheat for next year."

"The garden will be bigger next spring," Hannah added. "More food for my growing family."

"I hope the winter isn't too hard on several of my older patients," Gina said. "Some have arthritis, and one has gout."

"From all the signs, it should be an excellent trapping season," Ezra stated.

"I am going to learn to knit socks this year," Esther said shyly. "Ma has been teaching me."

Daniel, the quiet one, just listened while enjoying his big slice of pie.

On their way to Ezra's cabin, he and Gina talked about the day. "It's like I have a family again," she said softly.

"I have the same feeling," Ezra said. "Eban and Hannah have always been family to me."

"Thank you for attending church with me this morning," Gina said. "It meant more than you know."

Smiling, Ezra said, "Maybe we will do it again."

When they reached the cabin, Gina said, "Am I invited in for coffee?"

Taking her hands in his, Ezra said, "Do you have a busy day tomorrow?"

"I have the day off tomorrow," Gina said, gently placing her hands on his face and kissing him deeply. Their arms enfolded each other as they kissed, sure that each could feel the beating heart of the other. Ezra opened the door of the cabin, and they entered. Lighting an oil lamp, Ezra added firewood to the banked coals in the stove. As the cabin heated, they kissed, the long, slow, tender kiss of two people who knew their lives would change on this night. Holding Ezra's face in her hands, Gina looked deep into his eyes and whispered, "I love you."

Enfolding her in his arms, Ezra whispered, "And I love you."

The coffee would wait until morning.

CHAPTER ELEVEN

Ezra was skinning out the muskrats he had found in his traps. It was mid-morning, and a February thaw had melted much of the snow. During the day, the temperature rose into the high 40s and dropped back to the low thirties at night.

Sheriff Godfrey drove up to Ezra's in his Ford. As he and a deputy exited the car, Ezra noticed a grim look on the sheriff's face.

"What's wrong now, Luther?" Ezra asked.

"Two men just robbed the Burkesville Savings & Loan," Luther said. "Shot a teller and got away with $2300."

"Sounds like a job for the city police," Ezra said, "unless they managed to make it out of town."

"They took the highway west, but the train got to the crossing before they did," Luther said, "so they had to turn around. They blasted their way through a roadblock, killing a police officer. Their car got shot up, and we are pretty sure one is wounded."

Washing his hands at the pump, Ezra asked, "Did you find the car?"

Luther tipped his hat back on his head. "Yes, we found the car empty, with blood on the seat."

"Where is the car?" Ezra asked.

"On the dirt track behind Darnel Pruett's farm. Why they drove in there is a mystery."

Ezra thought for a moment and then raced toward the cabin. "I am going to change clothes and pack a few things. I'll be right back."

The first thing Ezra noticed were the plates on the abandoned car. "Minnesota plates. Explains why they were going west," Ezra said. "Looks like they were trying to get home."

"The people in the Savings & Loan said they were dressed like city boys," The sheriff said. "Hats, suits, overcoats, and shoes."

With a wry grin, Ezra said, "Not the best clothing choice if you are going into a tamarack swamp."

"You know this area?" Luther asked.

"Darnel had me trap some beaver out of here three years ago," Ezra explained. "There's about 5 miles of swamp before you reach Timm's Creek, which flows into the Flambeau River."

"How can we help?" Luther asked.

"Keep a deputy in a car parked right here," Ezra said. "Don't know how long it will take, but there is one way in and only one way out." Ezra removed a backpack from the sheriff's car, slipped it on, and inspected the ground. "Got a blood spot about every 10 feet," Ezra said. "One of them got hit, but not too bad. Might slow them down."

"Don't forget these guys are armed," Luther cautioned.

"So am I," Ezra said, patting the holster of his .45 Colt.

'Must be about noon,' Ezra thought as he started into the swamp. The robbers had tried to find the high ground, but very little could be found. A more prominent red blood spot appeared on a large tuft of grass. 'Must have taken a bullet in his side,' Ezra thought, 'an arm or leg wouldn't bleed that much.'

A patch of muddy, mashed-down moss and grass mixed with blood showed where the wounded man had fallen. The footsteps were getting closer together as the men tired out. About three miles into the swamp, Ezra stopped and listened.

Faint voices filtered across the wetland. Moving forward, Ezra found a bloody handkerchief in the mud. Due to the melted snow, the water was now knee-deep in places. Ezra could now track the sound of voices, which sounded angry!

"Stop, dammit!" one yelled. "I just lost my shoe!"

"Hurry up and find it," yelled another voice. Stepping carefully, Ezra moved ahead without a sound. Peering over a willow bush, Ezra saw them. One sat with his back against a tamarack stump, his left hand pressed to his side. Next to his leg was a canvas bag. The other man stood, shaking the mud out of the shoe he found. Drawing his Colt, Ezra stepped forward.

"Throw your guns in the water," he ordered. The two men stared in amazement; the one sitting reached into his overcoat.

BANG!

Ezra fired a shot at his feet. "Good way to get yourself killed." Turning to the man standing, Ezra said, "Put that shoe on. You will need it to walk out of here." Both men dropped their pistols in the water.

It was almost dark when Ezra got the two bedraggled

men to the dirt road, where a sheriff's car awaited. The deputy handcuffed both men and put them in the backseat. Carrying the bag filled with money, Ezra smiled and said, "Let's get these two taken care of."

Luther Godfrey was waiting at the Sheriff's Department. "Get the wounded man to the hospital and stay with him," he told the deputy. "I'll book the other one."

Ezra handed Luther the canvas bag. "No place to spend it," Ezra said, "so it should be all there."

"I've got some hot coffee for you," Luther said, "and I need you to tell me the whole story."

"Coffee first," Ezra said, "and keep my name out of the newspaper."

Regina Forrest rented a small house in Burkesville, just a block from the hospital. She stopped there every evening on her way home to replenish whatever supplies she had used on her rounds. She was standing at the counter with a nurse when a deputy came through the door holding a man in handcuffs.

"Got a wounded prisoner here," the deputy said. "He got shot in that robbery today." Another nurse came with a gurney and took the injured man to the emergency room. Having been out of town all day, Gina had no idea what had happened.

"Two men robbed the Savings & Loan this morning," the nurse told her. "Killed a policeman and almost got away."

"Who caught them?" Gina asked.

"Must have been the sheriff and his men," the nurse said. "That was a deputy with the injured man."

When her supply list was filled, Gina left the hospital and went straight to the Sheriff's Office. When she walked in the door, she saw Sheriff Godfrey and Ezra having coffee.

Ezra's eyes lit up when he saw her. "Hi Gina, what brings you here?"

"Are you alright?" she asked.

"I'm fine, but tired," he told her.

"Ezra was just about to give me his report," Luther said. "Have a seat and listen."

Ezra told what had happened and signed the statement for Luther. "If that is all you need," Ezra said, "I need some food." Ezra turned toward Gina. "If you haven't eaten yet, let's find a diner open and have supper."

"Don't you need a ride home?" Luther asked.

"I will take him home after we eat," Gina said with a smile.

They walked across the street from the Sheriff's Office to Molly's Cafe. The waitress, Lorna, came to take their order. "Hi Regina," she said with a smile. "You have company tonight. We have a stuffed pork chop and baked potato special that's really good."

"Bring us two," Gina said, "and coffee to start."

As the waitress left, Ezra said, "I'm not carrying any money."

"This is my treat," Gina said with a smile. "Just eat and enjoy."

After the meal, they walked to Gina's car, arm in arm.

"Long drive to my cabin and back," Ezra said.

"We are not going to your cabin," Gina said with a grin. "I'm taking you to my home. You will sleep there tonight, and I will take you home in the morning."

In Gina's car, Ezra asked, "How did you know I would be in the Sheriff's Office?"

"Whenever the sheriff needs help, he calls on you," Gina said. "When I saw that deputy bring in that wounded man, I knew you were involved. Did you shoot him?"

"No, he got shot running the roadblock," Ezra sighed, "and killed a police officer."

"Don't you ever worry about getting shot?"

Thinking a moment, Ezra said, "Never thought about it."

The newspaper did a big story about the robbery. When interviewed by a reporter, the sheriff referred to Ezra as 'a local citizen' but would not give out a name. People at the Crossroads knew it had been Ezra and just smiled when they read the story. About a week later, Luther met Ezra at the Crossroads store. "Got a check for you," he said. "The Savings & Loan offered a $500 reward for the capture of the robbers and the return of the stolen money."

"Did the policeman who was killed have a family?" Ezra asked.

"A wife and a baby girl," Luther answered.

"Give them the money," Ezra said, "and keep my name out of it."

"I think it's time I learned to drive an auto," Ezra told Nathan.

"Are you planning on buying one?" Nathan asked.

"No. But there are times when knowing how to drive would come in handy."

They were standing by Nathan's new Dodge. Opening

the door, Nathan said, "Sit behind the wheel, and I will get in the other side."

Gingerly, Ezra slipped into the front seat and looked down at the pedals. "Which is which?" he asked Nathan.

"From left to right, they are the brake, the clutch, and the gas pedal," Nathan said. "The lever on the side of the steering wheel is for changing gears."

"I've watched you drive," Ezra said, "so I have a rough idea what to do. How do I start it?" The first few tries went as Nathan expected. The Dodge would hop forward and stall out. Eventually, Ezra got the right amount of clutch and gas pedal footwork and then learned to shift the gears. Nathan was patient, never getting excited or raising his voice. Within an hour, Ezra was driving and smiling as he did so. Parking the Dodge back at the store, the two men sat for a moment.

"You did well," Nathan said, "but you could use a few more lessons."

"Maybe one more," Ezra said, "probably next week when I stop for the mail."

CHAPTER TWELVE

Spring finally arrived, and with it came the rain. The old stagecoach stop had been turned into a school, though the cedar shake roof needed replacing. The day after school was dismissed for the summer, eight local farmers showed up and began removing the old roof.

"Got more boards that need replacing," was the cry heard about every half hour.

"Just keep track of how many," Eban told the men. "Conner will cut what we need at the sawmill." As the old boards and shakes were hauled away to be used as firewood, the school board met to review the progress and estimate the cost.

Hiram Kruetzer, the board chairman, said, "The tar paper and new asphalt shingles will cost $300, which the board can cover. However, the new boards for the roof will cost another $150, which we do not have. Somehow, we need to raise the extra money to proceed." Almost to a man, the members shouted, "My money is tied up in spring planting!" The meeting ended with much grumbling and promises of "I'll see what I can do."

"I need a large can of coffee, sugar, and salt," Ezra told Rose. Nathan just finished emptying the ashes from the wood stove. "Should be the last time until fall," he said, wiping a sleeve across his brow.

"Good fertilizer for the garden," Ezra said.

"You missed a rowdy school board meeting, Ezra," Nathan told him.

"Who got rowdy?" Ezra asked.

"Everybody. We don't have enough to pay for the new boards for the roof of the schoolhouse."

Looking around to ensure they were alone, Ezra said, "Let's go outside and talk." Once on the porch, Ezra turned toward Nathan. "How much do the boards cost?"

"Conner can get them for us for $150," Nathan said, "but extra money is scarce during planting time."

"How much is in my account?" asked Ezra.

"Without looking," Nathan said, "about $500, give or take $20."

"Take out what they need for the boards, but on one condition," Ezra told him, "they don't know where you got the money."

"Why don't you want them to know?" Nathan asked.

With a sigh, Ezra explained. "If they don't know where the money came from, they won't be back asking for more."

Nathan laughed. "By God, you're right! Hiram Kruetzer would be after you every time they needed something."

"Probably best not to mention it to Rose, Nathan," Ezra said softly.

"I was just thinking the same thing."

After hard days of milking, planting, and milking again, the farmers from the Crossroads community rebuilt the schoolhouse roof, working until it was too dark to hammer a nail. The new boards were oak, without a single knothole. The Shipman Lumber Company had them delivered at no charge. By Thursday evening, the new boards were in place and ready for the shingles.

The rain held off Saturday morning, allowing the ten-man crew to lay shingles. Each sixty-pound bundle had to be carried up a ladder; among the men helping was Ezra Mulvey.

About 11:30, the women began arriving and set up sawhorses with boards across them to hold the food they had made for the hungry men. Nothing special, but tasty and filling. Ham and cheese sandwiches on fresh-baked bread, dill pickles, potato salad, coffee, cider, and cake for dessert. The women called it a 'save your fork' lunch to eat the cake with.

Regina Forrest stopped to see what progress had been made. The women insisted she stay and eat, pressing a plate of food into her hands. Because of the work she did on their behalf, Gina was special to each of them.

As the sun began its slow slide into dusk, the roof was done. No more wet students and ruined books. The few boards left over would be made into shelves along the walls. All the odd ends of cut shingles and tar paper were picked up, and the ground was raked for any nails. Then, one by one, the men went home, tired but happy.

"I had Lorna at the cafe pack us a lunch," Gina said, holding up a large wicker basket and smiling. Ezra had the horses saddled, with a blanket tied behind his saddle.

"The flowers should be in full bloom," Ezra said, helping Gina onto her horse. "I'll carry the basket."

Gina lifted a corner of the napkin covering the food, and Ezra inhaled deeply. "Fried chicken, one of my favorites," he said with a grin.

They were going to Gina's peaceful place, the little valley Ezra had shown her the summer before. The day was warm, almost 70 degrees, with only a light breeze from the west. As they rode, Gina chattered on, and Ezra listened, lost in the sound of her happy voice. She told him about the patients she had seen and how they responded to her treatment. She marveled at the new drugs coming to doctors and hospitals and how they helped save lives. Ezra smiled and nodded, with an occasional "that's wonderful" or "gosh sakes" to let her know he was listening. And then they were there.

"I call this place Gina's Valley," Ezra said as he spread the blanket on the ground. Gina blushed and wrapped her arms around him. Ezra tipped her lovely face up and gently kissed her.

"Are you going to pick some flowers?" he asked.

"Oh no," Gina replied. "The flowers belong where they are. We must not take away any of the beauty." They strolled down to the creek, her hand gently brushing the flowers as they passed. The birch trees were leafing out, the leaves a soft green. A startled grouse with several young chicks scurried away into the woods. Walking back, hand in hand, Gina mused, "Gina's Valley."

As they ate, they talked of their families. Gina recounted her father, Bascom. When he arrived home in the evening, they sat down to dinner, and then later, Bascom would read her a story from one of her books. Her mother, Katherine, was the guiding force in her life, encouraging her to try new things.

"We loved each other very much," Gina said wistfully. Ezra told her what he remembered about his mother and the gypsy lifestyle of his trapper father, Bertram.

"I wish you could have met my younger brother, Micah," he said. He told Gina about Micah taking his rifle apart, cleaning it, and putting it back together. Sadly, Ezra told the story of how Micah had died.

"Someday," Ezra said, "I would like to visit where he is buried to pay my respects to a real hero." When the chicken and salad were gone, it was time for dessert. Two slices of peach pie washed down with a bottle of root beer.

The slow-moving sun cast long shadows as they packed up to begin the ride home. Standing beside her horse, Gina gazed at the beauty spread before her.

Turning to Ezra, she said, "When my time comes to depart this earth, I would like to be buried in a place as lovely as this."

Ezra gently put his arm around her shoulder. "And I would be there with you." They held each other gently for what seemed like forever, then kissed. Mounting their horses, they rode slowly home.

"The county has decided we need a telephone," Nathan told Rose. "A crew is already setting poles to string the wire."

"That is a wonderful idea," Rose said, "but what will it cost us?"

"We will buy the telephone for $25," Nathan said. "The monthly service charge is $5."

"How long before the poles and wire reach us?" Rose asked.

"At the rate they are going," Nathan said, "I expect them to be here by next week if the weather holds." Having learned a lesson from the telegraph people, the poles holding the telephone wire were coated with creosote, a substance made from coal-tar that protected against weather and insects. Three crews were working: the hole-diggers, the pole-setters, and the wire crew. It was not a race, just a steady progress by workers who knew their jobs.

On Monday morning, three men entered the store. A tall, sandy-haired man held out his hand. "My name is Elgin Banks. We are here to install your telephone." One of the men behind him held the large wooden telephone tightly; the other man carried the necessary tools. "Where would you like it placed?"

Rose pointed to a space on the wall at the end of the counter. "This is where it will be most handy for us and the customers," she said.

The telephone was a marvel to behold. On one side was a metal hook that held the receiver. On top was a bell that rang when a call was coming in. On the front was a tube to speak into, and on the other side was a small crank.

"The wood is mahogany," Elgin said proudly. "It will last forever." A line from the pole set in the yard was fed through a hole drilled in the store's wall and attached to the telephone. "Now I am going to test it," Elgin said. He picked up the receiver and turned the crank. After a moment, he said, "I am testing the telephone we just installed at the Crossroads Store. Please call back." Then hung up the receiver. The bell atop the box rang almost immediately; Elgin picked up the receiver and handed it to Rose. Holding the receiver to her ear, Rose spoke into the tube. "Crossroads Store. Yes! I can hear you. Thank you!" she said.

Progress had come to the people of the Crossroads community.

CHAPTER THIRTEEN

To a farmer, the first cutting of hay marks the first day of summer. The smell of new-mown hay is intoxicating; it makes grown men smile like little boys. Some of the Crossroads farmers now used tractors for most of the heavy work, but a team of horses was often used for mowing. Tractors were noisy and smelled of gasoline, oil, and hot exhaust.

The mowing machine made a unique sound, a 'snick, snick, snick' as the sickle blade worked. The aroma of cut tall grass filled the air, swath after swath fell. After a day to dry, the hay rake would turn the swaths into windrows, and later, the hay-loader would fill the wagons with hay. Each farmer knew how much his cows and horses needed for the winter. With a bit of luck, three cuttings would fill the bill if the weather cooperated. As with all farm work, there was the possibility of an accident. Making hay, cutting firewood, stringing fence wire, or wrestling an angry bull all could end badly.

Regina Forrest had started her working day in the gray light of dawn. She picked up a list of people to see from the hospital duty nurse, grabbed a quick cup of coffee, and was on the road. A cow had stepped on a boy's foot, no broken bones but torn skin. A woman had scalded her hand in boiling water. A man with a swollen knee from where a horse had kicked him – the list filled a whole page, and each would be seen, along with any other mishaps.

The farmers and their families respected her work, offering her breakfast and lunch. Gina learned about each of them, and new ones were added almost daily. The women noticed a change in Gina over the past year. She seemed happier, more relaxed, and eager for any new challenge. 'She is seeing Ezra Mulvey,' they whispered among each other, and not one had a bad word to say.

There wasn't a family in the Crossroads community that Ezra had not helped. They all knew that Ezra had paid for the boards for the new schoolhouse roof. They also learned about the venison for the Schwanke family at Christmas – every time Ezra helped someone, they knew and quietly held him in high regard. If Ezra had chosen to court Regina Forrest, she must be an extraordinary woman.

Just before noon, Regina drove into the Thorne's yard just as Hannah finished hanging out the wash. She smiled and waved as she carried the empty basket to the front porch. "You are just in time for lunch," she said. "Come in and sit."

"How are my chicken-pox boys doing?" Gina asked. Both Jacob and Daniel had come down with the pox the same day. Esther had already been through it, and Noah showed no sign of it.

"Cranky and miserable," Hannah said with a grin, "but this will pass." Gina checked both boys, who soon would be better.

"Leftover biscuits and gravy today," Hannah said, "hope you like it."

Laughing, Gina said, "I would drive across the county for your biscuits and gravy."

As they ate, Hannah asked, "Have you and Ezra made any future plans?"

Pausing a moment, Gina said, "We know we are in love and will be together someday. How we plan to do it takes up much of our conversations."

With a smile, Hannah patted Gina's hand. "Getting him to talk and think about it is a huge step for Ezra. Be patient and honest with him, and God will find a way for you."

Ezra cut his hay with a scythe. The back-and-forth swing with the sharp blade easily took the tall grass down. Sweep and step, sweep and step. It was the way early farmers had done the work. The steady swing of the heavy scythe soon brought a sheen of sweat to Ezra's upper body.

The sun in a cloudless sky would soon dry the hay, and tomorrow, Ezra would turn it over with a pitchfork. When it was dried, the horse would haul it to the barn on a light dray for winter storage.

Taking a break, Ezra worked the pump, running cold water over his head and upper body. As he was drying off, Nathan Thorne drove up and got out.

"Any farmer around would gladly mow that for you," Nathan said, "but you are too stubborn to ask for help."

Grinning, Ezra stretched and said, "Don't need no help. I need the exercise."

Reaching into his pocket, Nathan handed Ezra an envelope. "The county is raising the property tax again," he said, "this is your notice."

Ezra read the notice, then folded and stuffed it into his pocket. "They want another five dollars for doing nothing," he scoffed. "They probably hit you and Rose harder because of the store."

Nodding his head, Nathan said, "Ours went up fifteen dollars, and Foley got hit with ten."

"And they never tell you where the money is going," Ezra said, "or why they need it."

Nathan smirked. "If they told people the truth, we could watch public whippings in the town square."

They both burst out laughing and were still laughing as Nathan drove away.

Foley Thorne was at his best when shoeing horses. When Foley began taking off the old shoes, the big draft horses seemed to know they were in good hands. "Steady boy," Foley said softly to the Belgian horse as he picked up a hind foot. The horse belonged to his brother, Eban, who lit his pipe as he watched Foley work.

"My oldest boy, Daniel, seems to have a way with horses," Eban said. "He's not tall enough to harness them yet, but I let him drive the team sometimes."

"Horses know who likes them," Foley said, "and they respond accordingly." Eban had bought his matched pair of Belgians when he mustered out of the Army after the war. He also owned a tractor, but the team was his pride and joy. Holding up one of the horseshoes he had removed from the Belgian, Foley studied it briefly, then began working the bellows on his forge. Within two hours, the team was shod.

Wilford Lang knew all there was to know about building a barn, or so he told Conner Lundtz. Listening patiently until Wilford ran out of knowledge and advice, Conner said, "How many barns have you built, Wilford?"

Momentarily stumped, Wilford finally said, "I don't have to build one to know how it's done. I just know how to do it."

"In that case, you don't need me," Conner said. "Hire your own crew and get to building."

At 52 years old, Wilford was average height and going to fat. "I'm a busy man," Wilford blustered. "I don't have the time to build a barn; that's why I want to hire you."

"Well, Wilford. I will build it on two conditions. First, I will build it my way, from start to finish. Second, do not interfere with me or my crew in any way. If you do, I will stop work, send my crew home, and bill you for the work completed."

Removing the straw hat that covered his bald head, Wilford sighed. "Doesn't sound like I have much of a choice."

"You have a choice," Conner told him. "Hire me or fire me."

Quite red in the face now, Wilford replied. "The only other barn builder around is Victor Mancel, and he is 50 miles away and charges more than you do. Go ahead and start building, but I'll be watching."

"You may watch from a distance," Conner said. "My crew will be here tomorrow morning to begin work."

Gina Forrest was at the Burkesville Hospital picking up her list of patients to see that day. A pick-up truck rolled to a stop by the front door, and two men stumbled out. Both were pale and sweating, barely able to walk.

"I need some help," the duty nurse yelled. "Bring two gurneys!"

Two orderlies appeared pushing gurneys ahead of them. When Doctor Nelson arrived, Gina was helping get the men loaded onto the gurneys. Closely examining both men, he mumbled a curse, then said, "Lead poisoning. With these two, that makes five cases within 24 hours."

Her eyes wide with alarm, Gina asked, "Have any women or children been admitted with this condition?"

"They are all men," Doctor Nelson said, "so I believe the cause would be tainted homebrew. I will know more after I do some lab work and talk to these two."

"What can I do to help?" she asked.

"While making your rounds, talk to the families about who may be making and selling moonshine. The women will probably know more than the men." Gina nodded and left the hospital, determined to get to the bottom of the lead poisoning.

Doctor Nelson was right. Lydia Johnson, the wife of Elmer Johnson, had a younger brother, Douglas, who worked at the Shipman Lumberyard. "Dougie stopped by last Friday and showed me a quart mason jar of what he said was moonshine. I asked him where he got it, and he said two men were selling it from the trunk of their car, which was parked on the road just off the lumber yard property."

"Did he drink any of it?" Gina asked.

Wiping her flour-covered hands on her apron, Lydia smiled. "Never got a chance. I poured it out on the ground.

Did he ever yell! 'I paid $3 for that!' he hollered. I gave him $2 back, which I had in my apron, and kept the jar."

"Do you still have the jar?" Gina asked.

"It's on the shelf in the mudroom," Lydia said. I haven't had a chance to wash it out yet." Lydia got the jar and handed it to Gina. There was still a tiny amount of liquid in the bottom of the jar.

"I will buy it from you," Gina offered. She handed Lydia $2 from her bag. "Doctor Nelson can analyze this, and if it is the tainted liquor, we can stop the men who are selling it."

Back at the hospital, Gina paced the floor in the waiting room. She had given the mason jar to Doctor Nelson, who said he would take it into his laboratory. "It'll take me about 20 minutes to analyze," he said. "One of the men who came in today said he bought some home brew out by Shipman's Lumberyard. Be patient and bear with me, and I'll run some tests."

As they talked, a woman and a boy came in the front door, supporting a man who kept mumbling, "I think I'm dying." With help, the man was laid on a gurney and rolled quickly down the hallway.

Although it seemed much longer, Gina had to wait fifteen minutes. Doctor Nelson returned with the results. "The amount of lead in the jar shows beyond a doubt that the moonshine poisoned these men," he said. "The sheriff must find and stop these men before someone dies!"

The doctor turned toward the duty nurse. "Trudy, call Sheriff Godfrey and have him come to the hospital as soon as possible."

Gina told the sheriff just what Lydia Johnson had told her. "That path is an access road off the county road," Luther said. "I can block both ends, arrest the men, and impound their car and anything in it."

"Be careful, Luther," Gina said. "They may be armed."

"So am I," Luther said, his hand resting on the butt of his revolver.

The arrest went off without a shot fired. The two men were from Wood County. It was their first time making and selling whiskey, and neither drank. They were simply out of work and trying to get by. When Doctor Nelson told them about the lead poisoning, they turned white, and one began crying. At trial, each got a five-year prison sentence. Gina Forrest received an award from the town for her active role in helping save lives. All the men recovered and swore off liquor for good. One told his wife, "From now on, it's just beer for me."

Hannah and Eban invited Ezra and Gina to go fishing on Sunday afternoon at Otter Lake.

"We will take Daniel in the boat," Ezra offered. Eban and Hannah took Jacob while Esther fished from the dock with Noah. The bass, sunfish, and bluegills were biting on red worms. By 4 o'clock, it was time to call it a day.

"We have more than enough for a fish fry," Hannah declared. "Nathan should have the coals going under the grill." They packed up and drove to the Crossroads. Ezra helped clean the fish while Gina and Rose rolled out the dough for biscuits. Hannah chopped cabbage for coleslaw.

Eban and Daniel had gone home to do the milking, returning as the first batch of fish came off the grill.

'I have a family again,' thought Gina as the talk and laughter flowed around her. Ezra caught her eye and winked at her. She winked back and laughed with joy.

CHAPTER FOURTEEN

"I don't need to see no darn doctor," Bill Brunner told his wife, Maggie. "That county nurse that comes around can take care of it." Bill had been rebuilding the roof on the chicken coop and managed to step on a nail. The rusty old nail went right through the sole of his work boot and into his foot.

"Dammit," Bill cursed. Lifting his foot, he pulled out the nail and returned to work. When Maggie noticed he was limping that night, she asked why.

When Bill told her, she made him soak his foot in hot water. The next day, he was still limping. "I want you to go in and see the doctor," she told him again. But Bill was a stubborn man.

Gina Forrest was making her rounds, and Maggie told her about Bill still limping after three days.

"That nail hole is red and swollen with pus," Maggie said.

The two walked out to where Bill was working on the chicken coop. "Hello, Bill," Gina called to him. "Maggie wants me to look at your foot."

Grumbling, Bill agreed and limped to the house. Wincing with pain, Bill took off his boot and sock. Examining his foot closely, Gina said, "Bill, the sole of your foot is infected, and you may have blood poisoning." Gina showed Maggie the tiny red lines around the wound. Maggie stood, pointed her finger in Bill's face, and said, "You are going to the hospital RIGHT NOW!" Knowing he was beaten, Bill let out a heavy sigh and nodded his head. Gina wrapped the foot, helped get Bill into their truck, and promised to check on him later when she finished her rounds.

Doctor Nelson slowly shook his head and adjusted his glasses. "If you had let this go just one more day, blood poisoning would surely have set in," he said. "As it is, you have a serious infection."

"Can I walk on it?" Bill asked.

"No, you cannot," the doctor told him. "I will give you a shot now and another in four hours. I will keep you overnight, and if the foot looks better tomorrow, you can go home. I will give Maggie some antibiotic pills for you to take, but no walking around for a week!"

Still, the same stubborn old Bill said, "I got a farm to run, cows to milk, and chores to do. I can't be sitting in the house for a week!" Doctor Nelson sighed, pulled up a chair, sat down, and looked Bill in the eye.

"Can you do all that on one foot?" he asked Bill.

At a loss for words, Bill just stared back. "Are you saying I could lose my foot?"

Without batting an eye, Doctor Nelson stated, "Not just your foot, Bill, but your lower leg as well. That's how fast blood poisoning spreads." This got Bill's attention.

"I guess I can hire someone to do the chores for a week," he said. "I sure don't want to lose my foot or my leg."

The doctor stood, placed his hand on Bill's shoulder, and said, "If you do exactly what Miss Forrest, Maggie, and I tell you, you will be walking around in no time."

Sunday morning, after church, Ezra and Gina were having coffee on the bench outside Ezra's cabin. Gina had told him about Bill Brunner and the nail.

"I'll stop around to see Bill tomorrow," Ezra said. "He can be stubborn, but he is not stupid. There are probably a few things I can do to help him."

Leaning over, Gina kissed his cheek and said softly, "You are a wonderful man, Ezra Mulvey."

Patting her knee, Ezra gruffly said, " Just keep that to yourself; I don't want people to get the wrong idea about me."

She giggled. "Your friends already know; the rest only suspect."

That afternoon, Gina and Ezra packed a blanket, some sandwiches, and a thermos of iced tea and rode out to Gina's Valley. As they dismounted, Gina said, "It never changes, Ezra. My little valley always seems to be the same beautiful place as when I first saw it."

Ezra spread the blanket on the grass and sat cross-legged. "When I first found this place, I knew it was special; that's why I bought you here."

Gina hugged him with the tenderness reserved for lovers. Ezra kissed her. "I'm hungry. Let's eat."

Laughing, Gina sat and unwrapped their meal. "I've told you all about my mom and dad, and you told me about your dad and brother but hardly anything about your mother."

"I don't know much about my mother, but Pa told

me a few things. He said he met Flower while trapping up around Bayfield. He said she was living with her mother and a French-Canadian trapper. When Pa left that spring, Flower packed her few things and went with him."

Unwrapping a sandwich, Gina asked, "Did they get married?"

"I don't think they did," Ezra said. "If so, Pa never mentioned it."

Gina poured iced tea into a cup. "Was she a good cook?"

"She did wonders with wild game," Ezra said with a slight smile. "In winter, Pa set out rabbit snares, and she made stew. Venison was what she was really good at. She liked to cook it outdoors over a bed of coals."

"Did you and Micah miss her when she left?" Gina asked.

Ezra sighed. "For a few months, we did miss her, then we both got busy taking care of each other. We didn't really understand why she left. We just accepted it and moved on."

Tears formed in Gina's eyes, and she reached for Ezra's hand. "I wish things had been better for you growing up," she said softly. Ezra pulled his handkerchief from his back pocket and gently dabbed at her tears.

"My childhood made me who I am today," Ezra said. "If it were different, then I might be different. It made me who I am."

Gina climbed across the blanket to hug Ezra, tipping over the thermos and squashing a sandwich with her knee. She hugged him fiercely and whispered, "I love you just as you are, Ezra Mulvey. Don't ever change."

Ezra had just stepped outside his cabin with his early

morning coffee. A golden yellow sun was slowly emerging through the gray mist.

KRACK!

Startled for a moment, Ezra thought, 'Somebody shooting with a .22 rifle.'

KRACK!

Ezra now knew where the shooting was coming from. 'Better check it out,' he thought. Saddling his horse, Ezra rode out. About fifteen minutes later, he heard voices, dismounted, and quietly approached two teenage boys standing over a downed deer.

"We can't take it home. Pa would tan my hide," one said.

"What do we do with it?" said the other.

Ezra rode out from behind the trees. "First thing you do is gut it out."

Taken by surprise, the boys stared at him with open mouths. The one holding the single shot .22 started to bring it up slowly.

"Drop the rifle, boy," Ezra said, his hand resting on the butt of his Colt revolver. Finally realizing the trouble he was in, the boy dropped the rifle. "What are your names?"

The boy who dropped the .22 said, "I'm Joe Klein, and this is my cousin, Fred Rausch."

Looking closely, Ezra smiled and said, "Mitchell Klein is your pa?"

Young Joe swallowed hard and looked pale. "You know my pa?"

"I sure do," Ezra said, "and I agree. Mitch would tan your hide, so you and your cousin will gut this deer and take it home."

Mitchell Klein was watering a team of horses at the trough when Ezra rode into the yard at the Klein farm. The boys had gutted the doe and helped Ezra load it behind his saddle.

"Morning Mitch," Ezra said with a smile.

"Morning to you, Ezra," Mitchell said. "What's with the deer?"

Ezra looked down at Joe. "Tell your pa about the deer."

Mitchell listened as Joe related the events, and then he removed his hat, scratched his bald spot, and replaced his hat. "Joe, you and Fred go wait in the woodshed; I will be there shortly."

Ezra dismounted and handed Mitchell the .22 rifle he had been holding. "Thanks for bringing them home, Ezra. Joe was probably showing off for his cousin, Fred, who is visiting for a week from Iowa."

"Boys will always be boys," Ezra said with a grin.

"I don't need the meat right now," Mitchell said, "but I hate to see it go to waste."

"It just so happens I know a family who can use it right now," Ezra told him. "They have been down on their luck, and the venison will help." Mounting his horse, Ezra said, "I wish I could stick around and watch the fun in the woodshed, but I got hot coffee waiting at home."

Mitchell laughed, saying, "I've got a new willow switch that needs trying out. Thanks again, Ezra."

Ezra dropped the venison off for Tom and Connie Bidwell and their two children, then rode home. The sun was out in full force now under a cloudless sky.

'We could use some rain,' Ezra thought.

He unsaddled and staked the horse out on a long lead. He was building a new corral, which would take up most of his day. Pouring another coffee, Ezra sipped it and thought back on the morning. He could have let the boys go and taken the deer, but that was not his way.

'The hard lessons in life are the ones you remember,' he thought, drinking his coffee in peace.

CHAPTER FIFTEEN

Not a drop of rain had fallen in almost two months. Most of the second crop hay was in, but it seemed more and more unlikely that a third crop would be harvested. Gardens could be watered, but not cornfields or hay fields. The small creeks used to water stock were bone dry, and the danger of wildfires was rising.

Then, as if God had heard a prayer, dark gray clouds began to gather. By late afternoon, the wind changed, and by evening, the first raindrops started to fall. There was no rolling thunder or flashing lightning to announce the life-giving water, no cloudburst or torrential downfall, just a slow, steady rain that would soak into the ground, where the moisture-starved plant roots would drink their fill. It was a 24-hour rain that, at times, slowed to a misty drizzle, then resumed its pace.

The sun rose the following day but hid behind the clouds. The air was cool, with only a light breeze to ruffle the dripping corn tassels. Toward evening, the rain slowed to a drizzle and, by evening, ended altogether.

Ezra took down the big wash tub hanging from the side of the cabin and set it on the bench by the pump. The smaller tub soon joined the larger one, and Ezra began filling them with water from the pump. Wash day!

There was water heating on the stove, and a large bar of lye soap was unwrapped. The washboard was hauled out and placed in the large tub. First, the sheets and towels were washed, rinsed, and hung on the line. Then, the work clothes were thoroughly scrubbed and rinsed.

Gina drove into the yard as the last shirt was hung up. She smiled as she got out of her car. "Next time you plan to do laundry, let me know, and I will bring mine along."

Laughing, Ezra said, "Your underwear hanging on my wash line would be front page news in the local paper."

Gina laughed as she hugged him, but then her face and eyes turned grave. "For the last week, I have been having some dizzy spells," she said. "Nothing real serious, but I was concerned. I had Doctor Nelson draw some blood and send it to the lab in Madison."

Ezra frowned. "Do you think it might be serious?"

Gina patted his chest. "I think I might need some iron pills or maybe more vitamins. I will know when the results come back from Madison."

"I think you work too hard," Ezra said. "Too many 12 and 14-hour days. You don't know when to slow down."

Gina grinned slightly. "A cup of your strong coffee always seems to help."

Linking his arm through hers, Ezra said, "The wash is done, and the coffee is hot. Come with me."

Doctor Nelson called Gina into his office early on Monday morning. "I am afraid I have some bad news," he told Gina. "Your blood test results are back." As Doctor Nelson thumbed through his papers, Gina could tell he didn't want to tell her the results but had to anyway.

"I am a grown woman," she said quietly. "I can handle any bad news you have for me."

Removing his glasses and sighing heavily, the doctor said, "Regina, you have leukemia. Do you know what that is?"

"Yes, I do," Gina said weakly. "We studied it in nursing school. It is a cancer of the blood. How advanced is my case?"

After a moment of silence, Doctor Nelson told her, "Your case is severe. I want to check you into the Mayo Clinic in Rochester, Minnesota as soon as possible."

Gina hung her head for a moment. "I have some things to do and some people to talk to before I leave."

Nodding his head, Doctor Nelson said, "I will call the clinic and tell them you will leave here early Wednesday morning. Will that be enough time?"

"That will be fine," Gina said softly. She rose from her chair and shook Doctor Nelson's hand. "It has been a pleasure working with you and your staff," Gina said. "I could not have wished for a better nursing experience."

After Gina had left the office, Doctor Nelson sat quietly for a few moments, then called the Mayo Clinic to make the appointment. After hanging up, he took a handkerchief from his desk and quietly wept.

Feeling faint, Gina stopped at Molly's Cafe. Lorna was there in a minute. She frowned as she looked at Gina. "My God, woman," she said, "you look like you need a week's rest."

Smiling, Gina said, "I'm just a little tired, Lorna. I would like a cup of hot tea and a small slice of pie."

"Molly made a tasty lemon custard pie. I'll cut you a piece." As Gina waited, she looked out the big window. Across the street, she saw a sign. 'Matthew J. Weddell, Attorney at law.' A plan took shape in Gina's mind, and she knew she must do it. When Lorna returned with the tea and the pie, Gina asked, "Do you know the attorney, Mr. Weddell?"

"I sure do. He eats lunch here almost every day. Why?"

"I need some advice about something," Gina said. "Is he someone you would trust?"

Lorna paused a moment. "If I had a legal problem, that's who I would talk to."

"As soon as I finish my pie and tea," Gina said, "I'm going to see Mr. Weddell."

Gina opened the door and stepped into Matthew Weddell's sparsely but tastefully furnished outer office. An older woman sat at a desk, talking on the telephone.

"We will call and let you know," she said and hung up the receiver. Turning to Gina, she smiled. "I'm Helen, Mr. Weddell's secretary. How may I help you?"

"I would like Mr. Weddell to draft me a will," Gina said.

"When would you like this done?" Helen asked. Gina explained her situation, saying, "I need this done as soon as possible."

Motioning to a chair by her desk, Helen said, "Please have a seat, and I will see if we can help you." The woman rose from her chair and stepped over to a door behind her. She knocked and entered. Almost immediately, she was back, holding the door open. "Mr. Weddell will see you," she said.

An older man of average build was seated behind a desk,

his brown hair graying at the temples. He wore glasses, which he removed as he stood.

"I'm Matthew Weddell," he said, holding out his hand.

"My name is Regina Forrest," she said, shaking his hand. "I need a simple will drawn up."

"Helen said there was some urgency," Matthew said. "Tell me more."

Gina explained her illness and said she was leaving for the Mayo Clinic on Wednesday.

"As of this moment, I am at your service," Matthew said. "Tell me how you would like your estate administered, and I will have Helen type it up."

Later, Gina packed what little she owned – a few clothes, toiletries, a picture album, and a journal since becoming the county nurse. Turning out the lights, she closed and locked the door. Her suitcase went into the backseat. She turned and looked at the small house, sighed, and got into the car. As she drove out of town, she tried to figure out how to tell Ezra she was leaving. Smiling to herself, she thought, 'Ezra would want the truth,' and that was what she would tell him.

CHAPTER SIXTEEN

Ezra was out gathering produce from his garden. In a basket, he had cucumbers, tomatoes, and some leaf lettuce. As Gina stopped the car and got out, Ezra held up the basket, saying, "You are just in time for a salad."

Gina walked up to him, put her arms around him, and laid her head on his chest. With a slight frown, Ezra dropped the basket, held her at arm's length, and looked into her eyes. "I know something is wrong," he said. "What is it?"

"Let's go in the cabin," Gina said. "I will tell you as we make the salad."

Gina stepped inside and sat at the table as Ezra set the basket down and sat next to her. "Dr. Nelson got the lab tests back from Madison," Gina said. "I have leukemia. Do you know what that is?"

Thinking a moment, Ezra said, "If I remember right, it is a blood disorder."

Nodding her head, Gina said, "It is commonly known as blood cancer. I have to go to the Mayo Clinic in Rochester, Minnesota on Wednesday to begin treatments."

Ezra sat, stunned, his hands clasped together. Finally, he asked, "How do they treat leukemia?"

Taking his hands in hers, Gina told him, "They will

give me quinine to fight the cancer, iodine or iron pills to replenish the blood, and morphine for the pain."

"Can it be cured?" Ezra asked.

With tears in her eyes, Gina said, "The survival rate is very low, but there is always a chance it can be cured."

"Are you in pain now?" Ezra asked.

"There is some pain," Gina said. "Some aspirin and some of your coffee would help."

Gina had a restless night, the pain ebbing and flowing through her body. Finally, at about 2 am, she drifted into sleep. Ezra stayed awake, watching her as she slept. With the first light of dawn, he arose, dressed, and made coffee. He heated water on the stove, knowing Gina would want to wash up. He fed and watered the horses in the corral, topping off the water trough. When he returned to the cabin, Gina was dressed and having coffee.

Holding her face tenderly in his hands, Ezra asked, "How is the pain?"

Smiling, Gina said, "I just took some aspirin, so I will be alright."

"You cannot drive to Minnesota by yourself," Ezra said. "We'll go to the store and ask Nathan to take us to the clinic."

"Do you think he will mind?" asked Gina.

"Nathan and Rose love you almost as much as I do," Ezra said. "They would be hurt if you did not ask."

"Also, I must talk to Hannah," Gina insisted. "She has been like a sister to me."

Hannah Thorne listened quietly as Gina told her about

the leukemia. She asked about treatment and nodded while Gina explained.

"Nathan will drive us to the clinic tomorrow," Ezra said. "We are going there next to ask, but I know he will."

Hannah sat quietly for a moment. "When Eban went off to war, I prayed every night that he would come home. Now you, Gina, will be in my prayers, asking God to bring you home." Both Hannah and Gina cried as they hugged.

In the car, Gina said, "I was never good at bringing people bad news."

Nathan and Rose were stunned when Gina told them. "Of course, I will drive you to the clinic," Nathan said, "and when the time comes, I will bring you home."

"Can you have visitors?" Rose asked.

"I will find that out when I check in," Gina said. "If so, I will tell Ezra."

"Where in Minnesota is this clinic?" Nathan asked.

"I know where it is," Gina said. "If we drive to LaCrosse and cross the river there, the clinic is just a few hours away."

"What about your car?" Rose asked.

"The car belongs to the hospital," Gina said. "We can drop it off tomorrow morning."

Nathan, Ezra, and Gina left the Crossroads store Wednesday morning at 5 o'clock. Ezra drove Gina's auto into Burkesville and left it in the lot behind the hospital.

"Those driving lessons paid off," Nathan said.

Gina was surprised, saying, "I had no idea you could drive."

"Nathan taught me," Ezra said, "in case I ever needed to drive, like today."

The traffic was light, with some delivery trucks and other cars on the road. By noon, they were in LaCrosse and crossed the Mississippi River. They arrived at the Mayo Clinic just before 2 o'clock.

The nurse on duty at the main desk smiled and said, "We have been expecting you, Miss Forrest. Please have a seat, and Doctor Blessing will be right with you."

Sitting in the waiting area, Gina reached into her purse and handed Ezra an envelope. Taking both his hands in hers, she said, "This is to be opened only if something unexpected happens."

"What is it?" Ezra asked.

"It is a will," Gina said softly. "I had it drawn up Monday. I hope and pray it is unnecessary, but I shall rest easier knowing it is in good hands."

Nodding slowly, Ezra folded the envelope and put it in his pocket.

The man striding down the hallway was medium height with silver-gray hair. His glasses did not hide his lively brown eyes, and his smile was friendly. As he approached, he held out his hand to Gina. "I am Doctor David Blessing," he said. "You must be Gina Forrest."

"I am," she said. "Nice to meet you." She pointed toward Ezra and Nathan. "These are my friends, Nathan Thorne and Ezra Mulvey."

Dr. Blessing shook their hands. "I hate to be so abrupt, but I need to get Miss Forrest checked in, take an x-ray, and do a complete physical today. This will allow us to begin her treatments tomorrow morning."

"Will she be allowed visitors?" Ezra asked.

"No visitors for the first month," Dr. Blessing said. "If, by then, she is responding to treatment, short visits will be allowed."

Gina turned, kissed Nathan's cheek, and hugged Ezra. "I will miss you so much," she whispered in his ear. Ezra's arms encircled her, not wanting to release her.

Finally, he slowly let go and said, "I will be back as soon as I can." Taking Gina's arm in his, Dr. Blessing led her away.

Nathan stopped at a roadside diner just outside of LaCrosse. Neither man had said a word since leaving the clinic. Both were lost in their thoughts, unable to express them.

"Could use some food," Ezra muttered.

"I need some coffee," Nathan said.

They took a corner table by the window. A man in a soiled apron came out of the kitchen and handed them a menu. "Waitress went home early," he said, "told me her feet hurt. The special is pork chops and mashed potatoes."

"Coffee first," Nathan said, "then two specials."

Sipping his hot coffee, Nathan said, "Rose is not going to be happy not being able to visit Gina."

Ezra nodded. "I feel the same way, but Gina needs time to concentrate on getting better."

The food arrived, and they ate. The man in the apron kept their coffee cups full and asked, "You want some apple pie for dessert?" They both said no to the pie, paid the bill, and left, ready for the long drive home.

The days passed with agonizing slowness. Ezra kept busy, cutting the last crop of hay. 'Might need to buy hay, with two horses to feed,' he thought. That afternoon, Ezra was working in the garden when he heard the team of horses and a wagon turn off the road into his yard. It was Abel Schwanke with a wagonload of hay.

With a big grin, Abel jumped down off the wagon. "This last load just would not fit in my mow," he said, "thought you might be able to use it."

Nodding his head, Ezra said, "Thanks, Abel. Pull around to the barn, and let's get it unloaded."

As the two men worked, Abel asked, "How is Miss Forrest doing at the clinic?"

"Haven't heard a word from the clinic," Ezra said, "which, I hope, means the treatments are working."

"When you see her, tell her me and the family pray for her every day," Abel said. Unable to speak, Ezra shook his hand and nodded.

As the empty wagon clattered away, Ezra looked out at the field where his two horses were staked out, munching on clover. 'Sometimes, a good deed comes back when you least expect it,' he thought.

On a Friday morning of the third week, Ezra was up early, as usual, when Nathan's Dodge drove into his yard. Nathan sat there for a minute, then slowly got out and walked up to Ezra. His eyes were red-rimmed, and his voice broke as he said, "J-just got a call from Doctor Nelson in Burkesville. Gina had a stroke early this morning, about 2 o'clock. She died, Ezra."

The cup of coffee slipped from Ezra's hand. His head slowly dropped to his chest, and his shoulders shook as the tears came.

"Doctor Nelson said the treatments had not done much good, and her heart just could not take the strain," Nathan said softly.

Ezra nodded his bowed head and wiped his eyes. "You go home now," he told Nathan, "Rose will be worried about you. I will come down to the store later."

Back in the cabin, Ezra opened the wooden chest at the foot of his bed. Before she left, Gina had left her journal and photo album here with Ezra, and this is where Ezra had put the envelope Gina had given him at the Mayo Clinic. He put the envelope in his pocket and went out to saddle his horse.

CHAPTER SEVENTEEN

Nathan and Rose were waiting for him as Ezra entered the store. Rose had been crying, and her red-rimmed eyes were still moist. She hugged Ezra. "I feel like we have lost a member of the family."

Ezra returned the hug, saying, "She was a member of our family, Rose, not by blood, but by heart." Turning to Nathan, Ezra held up the envelope. "Gina gave me this just before we left the clinic," he said. "It is her will. She told me to open it only if something happened to her. Would you call Doctor Nelson and tell him I would like to see him?"

"Of course I will," Nathan said, "but why?"

"I want to open this envelope with the doctor as a witness," Ezra said, "so there is no misunderstanding of Gina's last wishes."

"I will call right now," Nathan said.

Doctor Nelson was waiting for them in his office. Before him, on his desk, was an unopened envelope. "I can only imagine the loss you must feel with Gina's passing," he said, "and I am quite sure I know why you are here."

Ezra held up the envelope he carried. "Gina left this with me in case something happened."

Doctor Nelson held up the envelope from his desk and

said, "This was sent to me by an attorney here in town, Matthew Weddell. It is to be opened only upon the death of Regina Forrest."

Stunned for a moment, Ezra handed his envelope to the doctor. "Open this first and read it, then we will open yours." Sitting behind his desk, Doctor Nelson opened the envelope and unfolded the paper inside. After a moment, he said, "I am going to read this aloud for all of us to hear." Adjusting his glasses, he began . . .

"The final will of Regina Forrest:

I, Regina Forrest, being of well mind but ill health, feel it necessary to convey in writing my final wishes in the event of my death. I have a savings account at the Farmers & Merchants Bank of Burkesville in the amount of $975.00. This I leave to the Burkesville Hospital children's fund to be used as they see fit. I have little else to give except my journal and photo album, which I leave to my love, Ezra Mulvey.

When I have passed from this earth, I wish to be cremated. The ashes are to be placed in a metal container, sealed, and given to Ezra Mulvey for burial. He alone knows where I am to be buried. I wish I had more to leave to the Thorne family, who have taken me in and treated me as one of their own.

There are two copies of this will, one for Ezra Mulvey and the other for Doctor Nelson at Burkesville Hospital. This will settle any legal dispute as to my final wishes.

Signed, Regina Forrest
Witness, Matthew J. Weddell"

Doctor Nelson looked up from the will and said, "I will now open the envelope I received and read it." He opened the envelope, took out the paper, and read quietly. When he finished, he removed his glasses and wiped his misty eyes. "With your permission, Mr. Mulvey, I will take both copies of Gina's will and have them duly recorded at the courthouse. I will also contact the Mayo Clinic and have them carry out Gina's final wishes."

Ezra shook the doctor's hand. "Gina must have held you in high regard."

Nathan shook hands with the doctor, then he and Ezra left the office.

Hannah Thorne was tending her rose bushes when Ezra rode into the yard. As he stepped down from the saddle, Hannah walked to him and took his hands in hers. "Anyone who knew Gina is going to miss her," she said, "the Thorne family most of all." Ezra pulled her close and hugged her briefly.

Letting her go, he said, "I am waiting for the clinic to send me her ashes. I will bury her in 'Gina's Valley.'"

Hannah smiled. "Gina told me about her favorite place on earth and how she wished to be buried there."

"I am not going to put up a marker or stone," Ezra said, "but I would like to plant a rose bush for her if you could part with one of yours."

With a big smile, Hannah said, "I have a young rose bush just coming into bloom that would be perfect! Let me know the day, and I will dig it up for you."

Grinning, Ezra asked, "Does it come with an apple pie?"

"Esther has been asking what she can do for you," Hannah said, "she will bake you that pie."

It was ten days before the metal box of Gina's ashes arrived. Hannah helped to carefully dig up the rose bush. "The roots must be kept moist until it is replanted," she cautioned.

Esther proudly presented Ezra with a still-warm apple pie. "I wish there were more I could do," she said as she handed the dish to Ezra.

Ezra leaned down and kissed her forehead. "You are so much like your mother," he said softly.

When Ezra reached the valley, the sun was almost straight up. It was cool but not cold. Fall was coming soon. The leaves on the oaks and maples were just beginning to turn color, and the birches would soon follow. Many flowers were still in bloom, but the vibrant colors were muted as if they knew Gina would no longer be there to marvel at their beauty.

Ezra stood looking out over the landscape. 'Gina's Valley,' he thought, watching the breeze ruffle the flowers. He removed the rose bush and a short-handled shovel from behind the saddle. Choosing a spot, Ezra pushed the shovel blade in with his foot and began to dig. Soon, the hole was about 18 inches deep and a foot square.

From his saddlebag, he took the metal box of ashes wrapped in a piece of an old wool blanket. He held the box gently, not wanting to let go, but knowing he had to, he laid it in the hole. Reaching down, he removed some small rocks from the dirt, not wanting to hear them hit the box. The dirt soon covered the box of ashes, and he stopped shoveling.

Gently, he picked up the rose bush and centered it in the hole, packing the remaining dirt around it. From his saddle horn, Ezra unhooked a canvas water bag. He filled it in the creek, returned, and watered the roses.

'At least I could grant your final wish, Gina,' he thought. 'You gave me happiness I never dreamed I could have and gave me love I had never known.' A tear slid down his weathered cheek. Wiping it away, he packed up his shovel, mounted his horse, and rode home.

That evening, Ezra took out the photo album Gina had left him. Sitting at the table, he lit the oil lamp, turning up the wick a little more. Sipping a cup of coffee, he opened the album. He was greeted with a picture of a woman and a girl in her early teens. Smiling, he whispered, "Gina and her mother." The next image was of a medium-tall, stout man with a goatee. 'Must be her father, Bascom,' he thought. A picture of a two-story house and the final photo of another woman, 'Gina's Aunt Helen,' thought Ezra.

Along with the pictures was a newspaper clipping telling of Bascom's sudden death. Turning the page, more pictures: Gina and five other girls in white nurses' uniforms holding diplomas, another of Gina, her mother, and Aunt Helen together, a postcard showing the Blatz brewery, Gina and another girl, probably a friend, leaning on the front of a Ford Model-T. A few more postcards, a picture of a hospital, and then the pictures stopped. The last item was a headline from the Milwaukee Journal newspaper: WAR DECLARED!

Ezra slowly closed the album. His coffee had gone cold,

but he drank what little was left. He laid the album back in the chest, rinsed the coffee cup, added some firewood to the stove, blew out the lamp, and went to bed.

The morning was cold, hovering between 35 and 40 degrees. Ezra got the stove going and made coffee and biscuits from Hannah's recipe, topping them with honey. Halfway through the second biscuit, he heard a car drive in and, moments later, a knock on the door.

"Come on in, Luther," Ezra said.

"How did you know it was me?" asked the Sheriff as he entered.

"You still haven't oiled that squeaky hinge on your car door," Ezra said with a smile. "Sit down and help me eat these biscuits, and I'll pour you some coffee."

Luther took off his hat, laid it on the end of the table, and helped himself to a biscuit. "I just wanted to stop by and pay my respects on Regina's passing. I didn't know her well, but she impressed me by how she treated folks."

"She will be remembered by everyone she met," Ezra said. "The county was lucky to have her for the time they did."

"I also wanted to check on you," Luther told him. "Your friends worry about you."

Smiling, Ezra said, "No need to worry, Luther. I will be fine. I will miss Gina every day. The sorrow will pass, and the memories will never leave me."

CHAPTER EIGHTEEN

The sun was well up when Nathan drove into Eban Thorne's yard. Ezra and Eban came out on the porch, each holding a coffee cup. The Belgian horse team was hitched to a wagon loaded with saws and axes. "Thanks for the offer to help make firewood," Eban said with a grin. "It will make the work go faster."

"I don't get much exercise standing behind a counter," Nathan said. "I need to work off some extra weight."

Pointing at Nathan's middle, Ezra grinned and said, "If you grew a white beard, you could pass for Santa Claus." Laughing, the three men climbed into the wagon and set off for the woodlot.

"Foley got you and Rose converted to burning coal for the store," Eban said. "That must get dusty at times."

"Not really," Nathan said. "Foley always buys that hard coal they call anthracite and says it burns hotter and cleaner in his forge."

"Cost much?" Ezra asked.

"Cheaper than wood," Nathan said, "if you figure in the cost of labor and delivery, although I do miss the smell of hardwood burning on a cold morning."

Smiling, Ezra said, "I know what you mean. Sometimes,

I throw in a piece of pine just to hear the snap of a pine knot." Nathan and Eban nodded, knowing what he meant.

The trees they were cutting up had been felled last year and left to season. Ezra was cutting the limbs off the logs, swinging the axe with the precision of long practice. Nathan and Eban worked the two-man saw, cutting the logs into firewood lengths. As the sun rose, the men shed their long-sleeved shirts, stopping occasionally to wipe the sweat and sawdust from their faces with large cotton handkerchiefs.

When the sun reached its peak, they stopped for lunch. Hannah had packed a large paper bag with roast beef sandwiches and cinnamon buns left over from breakfast. A thermos of lukewarm coffee washed it all down.

The horses were led to the creek for water. Ezra had trimmed out some of the larger branches, cut them to length, and loaded them into the wagon.

"I'll spell one of you on the saw," Ezra offered.

"Hand me that axe," Eban said. The work lasted about two more hours, and all agreed it was time to load the wagon. With the sun beginning to slide down to the horizon, the team was hitched up and they headed home. This load of wood was for the farm; the next load would be for Ezra.

The horse Ezra had bought for Gina was now a pack horse. It would hold the supplies he needed for a 3-day trip to scout some trapping areas. Every trapper knew that if you trapped in the same area every year, soon it was trapped out. Ezra rotated his areas on a four-year schedule, always checking new places. If he found one he liked, he would check with the owner for permission.

Lately, the lynx population had increased, and lynx pelts brought good money. Muskrat and beaver were still plentiful, and an occasional bobcat was a plus. Ezra could read sign. Paw prints told what animal, how large, and the area they traveled. Tail drags and chewed trees meant beaver, and he was always on the lookout for muskrat houses. As he packed, he thought, 'Hope the bears leave me alone.' He hadn't seen any sign of bear yet, but it was best to be careful.

Ezra made camp at a site he had used two years ago. It was a small clearing on a low rise with a fast-moving stream just below. The fire ring of rocks was visible under a pile of leaves and twigs. Ezra unsaddled and unpacked the horses, let them drink from the stream, and then tethered them on long leads to eat. He cleaned out the fire ring, gathered dry wood, and soon had a blazing campfire. He filled the coffee pot with clear water from the stream, added coffee, and hung the pot from a tripod over the fire.

From his pack, he took out a 10-foot square section of tan canvas. With his hatchet, he cut a 12-foot-long pole and a 6-foot-long rod with a V-shaped end. The rod was driven into the ground about a foot. One end of the long pole was butted into the ground, the other end laid in the notch of the rod. Over this went the canvas. Ezra pegged the canvas down on the corners and the back, creating a shelter like an upside-down V.

Years ago, Ezra had used blankets to sleep on, but Nathan had sold him a sleeping bag, and he liked the comfort of the extra padding. The saddle and blanket rested on a two-foot-tall stump. When the coffee was ready, it was time to eat. He took out a frying pan from a canvas pack, some already-sliced bacon, and biscuits he had made that morning.

The sun was long gone, but a three-quarter moon gave enough light to eat by. There was no wind, and the smoke from the campfire rose straight up until it disappeared in the darkness. Content, Ezra sipped his coffee and chewed slowly on a bacon-filled biscuit. This was the life he knew and loved. When an owl hooted in the distance, Ezra cupped his hand over his mouth and hooted back.

Finishing the biscuits, Ezra rose, washed out the frying pan with sand at the creek, rinsed the pan with hot coffee, and then cleaned and refilled the coffee pot with water, ready for the morning. Ezra added a few more chunks of wood to the fire, knowing he would have warm coals at dawn. Taking off his jacket, he folded it and laid it in the sleeping bag for a pillow. Taking off the boots, gun belt, and hat, he slid into the sleeping bag and, within minutes, was asleep.

He awoke just before dawn and lay quietly, his thoughts about Gina. 'She would have loved to be with me here,' he thought with a slight smile. He would miss her every day, but every day would bring fond memories of their time together.

He rose, dressed, and stirred the ashes of the fire. A few glowing coals remained. He fed them with small, dry sticks until a flame appeared, then laid on more wood. Adding coffee to the pot, he hung it on the tripod. Leading the horses to the stream, he watched the sunrise. The air was cold but would warm up in a few hours. The coffee was ready. A quick breakfast of cold biscuits, then pack up the camp. The sleeping bag was rolled up, the canvas tent was taken down, and the packhorse repacked. The last of the coffee was poured on the fire, the coffee pot rinsed, and another pot of water poured on the campfire for good measure. Saddling his horse, Ezra looked around to ensure nothing was forgotten, then mounted and rode southwest. If all went well, he would be home by sunset.

By late afternoon, Ezra was on the game trail winding around Otter Lake. Reining in his horse, he thought a fish fry would be the perfect supper. He let the horses drink as he rummaged in his saddlebag for the fishline he always carried. Spotting a likely willow sapling, he cut, trimmed, and attached the line. A rotten log gave up some grubs for bait. In about a half-hour, Ezra had a bass, three sunfish, and two perch. 'Just enough for a meal,' he thought.

He mounted up, and within an hour, he was home. He unsaddled, unpacked, and set about cleaning the fish. The scouting trip had been worth it; tomorrow, he would check with the property owner he had selected. It looked promising, with signs of muskrat and maybe mink.

Ezra always fried fish in bacon grease for the flavor. After supper, he cleaned and re-oiled the cast-iron skillet and washed the dishes. 'A sleeping bag is fine,' he thought, 'but the bed will feel good tonight.' Adding some wood to the stove, he blew out the lamp and drifted off to sleep.

CHAPTER NINETEEN

It had been a very mild winter with good snow cover but only a few days of below-zero temperatures. The trapping had been good: a muskrat, three minks, a pine marten, two lynxes, and several beavers. While eating his breakfast of pancakes with maple syrup and hot coffee, something flew past the window. Ezra smiled softly. "If I'm not mistaken, that was a robin."

He got up, opened the door, and stepped out. On the arm of his bench, looking right at him, sat a big, red-breasted robin!

"You are a bit early," Ezra said to the bird, "but you are a welcome sight."

Just then, an unfamiliar car drove up his driveway. The car door opened, and a man Ezra had never seen before stepped out. He was of medium height, maybe 5 foot ten or eleven, stout, with a short brown beard that was going gray. The man was dressed casually in lace-up boots, khaki pants, a green plaid wool shirt, and a fedora hat.

The man smiled as he approached and held out his hand. As the men shook, the stranger said, "My name is Harlan DeWitt. You must be Ezra Mulvey."

"I am," Ezra said. "Coffee is hot; come on in and have a cup."

"I will," Harlan said, "and I have a whopper of a story to tell you!"

Ezra poured them both coffee and said, "Now, what is this story you have?"

Harlan grinned and said, "I worked a gold claim with your pa, Bert, in the Yukon."

Stunned, Ezra just sat there with his mouth open, unable to speak. Harlan sipped his coffee and said, "Before I continue, I must tell you your pa has passed away. It was two years ago. He got the lung fever and died at our cabin on the Stuart River."

"How did you two meet?" Ezra asked.

Harlan laughed. "That is a story all in itself. I am from a small town in Minnesota called New Ulm. When the newspaper mentioned the first gold strike, I was working on a farm as a hired hand."

"The first one?" Ezra said. "How many were there?"

"Three," Harlan said. "The first was in the Yukon, the second around Nome, and the third was Fairbanks. Me and Bert got in on the second one. When I read about more gold, I packed what I owned in a canvas bag, which wasn't much, and walked down to the freight yard, hoping to catch a train going west."

"I take it you were a bit low on cash," Ezra said with a grin.

"A hired man don't make much," Harlan said. "Forty dollars a month with room and board. I had $10 in change in my pocket, so I went looking for an empty boxcar with an open door."

Ezra poured them both more coffee. "You must have found one," Ezra said.

"I did," Harlan said, "but it wasn't quite empty. There was a man sitting on the floor against the wall, watching me. I tipped my hat and told him my name. He said, 'I'm Bertram Mulvey. Call me Bert.' He had an old leather satchel between his legs, wore boots, work clothes, and a battered Stetson hat."

"Pa left here in the early summer of 1901," Ezra said. "Is that when you met?"

Smiling, Harlan said, "That's right, it was June 1901."

"How long did it take you to get to Seattle?" Ezra asked.

Harlan reached into his shirt pocket and pulled out a pipe. "Do you mind if I light up?" he asked.

"Go right ahead," Ezra said. "I will make a fresh pot of coffee for us, then I want the whole story."

Harlan got his pipe going, stretched his legs, and crossed his ankles. "Nice cabin," he said, looking around.

"Pa, me, and my younger brother Micah built it just before he left," Ezra told him.

"Your brother lives here too?" Harlan asked.

"Micah got killed in the war," Ezra said, "back in 1918."

"Read about that war in the newspaper," Harlan said. "Glad I missed it."

"Tell me about your trip to Seattle," Ezra said.

"Well, sir, me and your pa rode that boxcar to Casper, Wyoming, where we got kicked off. Good thing, too, because the brakeman who kicked us off told us the train was headed to California."

"You must have been hungry and thirsty by then."

"We were," Harlan laughed. "We started walking and stumbled on a hobo jungle. They had a big pot of stew over a fire and told us to help ourselves, which we did."

"What kind of stew?" Ezra asked.

"Hobo stew," Harlan said. "Whatever anyone could spare went into the pot. Not real tasty, but it filled us up. We stayed the night, and the next morning, we walked into Casper. We stopped in a store and bought a loaf of day-old bread and some cheese. Walking out of town, we passed a gasoline station. A trucker was getting his tank filled with diesel, and your pa said, 'That truck has Idaho plates on it. Let's ask him for a ride.' We waited till the man came out of the station and asked him. He said he was going to Boise, Idaho and welcomed the company."

"What was he hauling?" Ezra asked.

"He had a load of cut lumber," Harlan said, "covered with a tarp. It was a bumpy ride on those mountain roads. That trucker, named Joe, talked all the way. Me and Bert made some sandwiches with the bread and cheese, and Joe talked while he ate, telling us his life story."

"Speaking of food," Ezra said, "I plan on a supper of bacon, beans, and some fresh biscuits. Be glad to share, and you can stay the night."

"Sounds great," Harlan said. "I'll get my things from the car while you start cooking."

When the biscuits were ready, Ezra dished up the beans and poured the coffee. "You must add something to these beans," Harlan said. "They taste wonderful!"

Smiling, Ezra told him, "I cook them with molasses and a touch of honey."

"Good biscuits too. You are some cook, Ezra."

"How did you get from Boise to Seattle?" Ezra asked.

"Joe dropped us off at the railyard in Boise," Harlan said. "There were three other guys waiting for the train to Seattle. We all waited in the shadows for a few hours until the train started moving and then jumped on. We went through more mountains and a few tunnels, and by the next afternoon, we were in Seattle."

"You must have been almost out of money by then," Ezra said. "How did you get passage?"

"We got work cutting firewood for the steamers," Harlan said. "Trucks would bring in logs, we would help unload them, cut them up, and split the wood. Paid good wages, and after two weeks, we had passage money and a little extra."

"How long did it take to get to Nome?"

Slowly shaking his head, Harlan said, "Not exactly sure, Ezra. The days all seemed to run together on the water. It was summer when we left Seattle and fall when we got to Nome."

"I'll bet you were anxious to get to the gold fields," Ezra said.

"We were," Harlan said, "but we needed a few things, like picks, shovels, and mostly food. We found a storefront that sold stuff other miners had got rid of when they left. We found most of what we needed, plus a used Winchester, and your pa bought a dozen traps for almost nothing."

Ezra nodded his head. "Pa was a trapper, and I bet those traps came in handy."

Harlan lowered his head a moment, then looked up. "Those traps saved our lives."

Ezra drained the last of the coffee. "It's getting late. Let's get some sleep, and you can tell me the rest tomorrow." Harlan had a sleeping bag and spread it over some blankets Ezra had laid on the floor by the stove. "If you get cold, add a few more pieces of wood to the fire."

Harlan unlaced his boots. "This is like old times. Many a night, me and Bert slept on the floor by a stove. I'll tell you about that tomorrow."

CHAPTER TWENTY

The sun rose in full force on a cloudless day. The robins, chickadees, and sparrows whirled and danced through the sunbeams, chirping their welcome to spring. Harlan woke to the aroma of fresh-brewed coffee. Ezra was at the stove, flipping pancakes and turning bacon.

"I slept the whole night through," Harlan said with a yawn. "I haven't done that in years."

"Slept good myself," Ezra said. "Hope you don't mind pancakes for breakfast."

"Love pancakes," Harlan replied, "especially with maple syrup."

"Got that," said Ezra, "and bacon on the side."

After breakfast, the men took their coffee outside. Sitting in the sun on the long wooden bench, Ezra asked, "When did you find gold?"

"Not until spring," Harlan said. "We left Nome and headed northeast toward Anvil Creek. There were hundreds of miners already there, staking claims. Bert and I pushed north, looking for the right spot. Then we discovered this feeder creek that ran into the Anvil. We staked it out and got out our gold pans. We got a few flakes of gold, just enough to keep us moving up the creek. After a week, we came to this small clearing with a cabin. It was empty and looked like it had been empty for quite a while."

"Was it a trapper's cabin?" Ezra asked.

"That's what Bert thought," Harlan said. "We decided to stop for a few days to take stock. The weather was turning cold, so we cut wood and lit a fire in the old pot-belly stove. Sure felt good to get warm."

"Did you have food with you?" asked Ezra.

"Rabbits," Harlan laughed. "Bert set out snares every day, and we ate rabbits. Anyway, we slept there, and in the morning, we awoke to a snowstorm! Luckily, we had brought in wood and water, so we made coffee and waited it out. The snow stopped sometime during the night, and by the next morning, we decided to stay until spring."

"I'll bet that's when Pa took the Winchester, the traps, and some bacon and headed out."

Laughing, Harlan said, "That's exactly what he did! I grabbed the axe and started cutting up dead trees for firewood. The creek had frozen, so I busted a hole in the ice with the axe and hauled water in an old wood bucket I found hanging on the outside wall."

"How long before Pa got back?"

"Got back that night," Harlan said, "dragging a deer. We skinned it out and ate venison for a week! Tasted mighty good."

"Did the trapping pay off for Pa?"

"Every day, he came back with something," Harlan said. "I had to cut and shape some wood to make a sled for him to haul his catch. Some of it we could eat, which helped."

Grinning, Ezra asked, "Any bears show up?"

"Never saw a bear," Harlan said, "but Bert did run across some moose. He shot one young one, quartered it, and made two trips to get it all back to the cabin on the sled. That was some good eating."

"I bet you were glad to see spring come," Ezra said.

Harlan laughed. "If we had stayed in Nome, we could have got rich! A prospector discovered that the beach was covered with gold! Men sifted the sand and took out as much as they could carry. By the time we got back, it was all over. What gold we found before the snow hit came to about $200. Bert sold his pelts for $500! With that money, I bought a Remington 20-gauge pump shotgun, and Bert bought a pack mule. We loaded up on supplies and headed out for the Stuart River."

"Was that another gold strike?" Ezra asked.

"Yes and no," Harlan said. "It was one of the big ones back in '97 that was played out by 1900. Then someone thought to move farther upriver in '03 and hit more gold. Bert and I got there early and happened on a good claim."

Looking up, Ezra saw the sun was right overhead. "We have talked the whole morning," he said, "and I bet you still have more story to tell."

Harlan grinned. "Want to hear about the claim jumpers?"

"I sure do, but I have a few chores first. I got two grouse I need to pluck and clean so I can fry them for supper."

"What can I do to help?" asked Harlan.

"I got some potatoes you can peel and cut up to fry and some canned green beans."

As they ate a leisurely supper, Ezra asked, "Did you stake a claim on the Stuart River?"

"We bought a claim," Harlan said. "We were headed upriver and passed a man outside a cabin digging a hole. We stopped and asked if we could help. The man, Zeke Kelsey, told us he was digging a grave for his partner, who had been shot by claim jumpers. 'If you men are looking for a claim, I will sell you this one, as I am quitting this country.' Bert and I looked at each other, nodded our heads yes, and Bert asked how much Zeke wanted for his claim."

'How much do you have?' Zeke asked.

'We have $200 in cash,' I said.

'Throw in that mule, and the claim is yours,' Zeke said. Zeke wrote out two bills of sale that all three of us signed, one for us and one he would file when he got to Nome. We helped Zeke bury his partner, then he packed in a hurry, loaded the mule, and left."

Pouring more coffee, Ezra asked, "How long before the claim jumpers returned?"

Grinning, Harlan said, "Three men came back that night expecting Zeke and got us. I stayed in the cabin, and Bert was outside. When they opened fire on the cabin, Bert shot at the rifle flashes and managed to wound two of the men. The other man took off."

"Pa was a good shot with a Winchester," Ezra said. "Did you take the men into Nome?"

Smiling, Harlan said, "Bert had a better idea. We stripped those two down to their underwear, tied their hands behind their backs, and sent them down the trail barefoot. Told them if they came back, we would hang them. They never came back."

"How long did you work the claim?"

With a sigh, Harlan said, "Almost 20 years we had that claim. Sometimes, weeks went by with nothing; then, we would hit a pocket of gold! Bert and I took turns shoveling and working the rocker. We hit one vein that seemed bottomless; then it just played out. Three weeks later, we hit another pocket!"

"Did you get rich?" Ezra asked.

Smiling, Harlan said, "There were times when we had over $25,000 in the bank in Nome. I was all for quitting and going home, but Bert convinced me to stay on. The thing was, the gold didn't really interest Bert. It was the freedom of living in the wild that kept him there."

Nodding his head, Ezra said, "That sounds like Pa."

"A few times, I would go into Nome for supplies," Harlan said softly, "and stay for a week just to have a good time. Then I would head back, and I swear Bert never knew I had been gone. It was like the land had a hold on him."

"Did he ever mention he had family?" Ezra asked.

"Bert talked about you and your brother sometimes," Harlan said. "He told me about this cabin and how he knew you would take care of Micah."

"Do you still have the claim?" Ezra asked.

"That is the reason I am here," Harlan said with a big smile. "When Bert died, I buried him on the hill behind the cabin. Then I went into Nome and sold the claim! A mining operation bought it for $20,000!"

Ezra let out a low whistle. "I moved back to New Ulm and bought a small ranch," Harlan said. "I raise Angus beef cattle now, make a good living. I decided it was time to look you up and give you the money Bert had in the bank and your half of the sold claim." Ezra stared at Harlan, not believing what he was hearing. Harlan laughed and handed Ezra a small brown book. "This is a bank book. It shows a deposit of $19,500 in your name in the First National Bank of Burkesville."

For the first time in his life, Ezra was at a loss for words. Finally, he grinned and then started laughing! He laughed so hard that tears ran down his cheeks. Finally, gasping for breath, he wiped his face and said, "Sorry about that, Harlan. It just struck me funny. My Pa, who seldom had two nickels to rub together, died a rich man."

CHAPTER TWENTY-ONE

The next morning, after breakfast, Harlan packed his bag. "It has been a real pleasure meeting you, Ezra. You remind me a lot of your pa." They shook hands and walked out to Harlan's car.

Then Harlan snapped his fingers. "I almost forgot; I have one more thing for you." Opening the trunk of his car, he took out a cloth-wrapped bundle and handed it to Ezra. "I thought you would like Bert's old Colt .45."

Ezra opened the bundle, revealing a worn leather holster with the Colt. Through misty eyes, Ezra said, "Pa taught me to shoot with this revolver. Thank you, Harlan."

"I want you to come visit me at my ranch someday." Nodding his head, Ezra assured him that he would. As Harlan drove away, Ezra stood in the early morning sunlight, still trying to take stock of all he had learned about his pa's life in the Yukon.

Getting the garden ready for planting gave Ezra plenty of time to think. As he shoveled and raked, he let his mind wander, not settling on any plan or idea.

'One thing I would like is an indoor bathroom,' he thought. Smiling, he wondered, 'Am I getting old and soft?'

At noon, he stopped for lunch: leftover pancakes smeared with honey and rolled up.

'Gina always said an indoor tub and toilet would be nice,' he thought. As he thought of Gina, an idea began forming in his mind. Then he grinned and clapped his hands.

'What a great idea,' he thought. He rolled it over in his mind and finally decided how to proceed. 'The first thing I need to do is let the Thorne family know about Pa.'

It was Friday. If he could get the families to meet at the store after church on Sunday, he could tell them then. 'The first one to ask would be Nathan,' Ezra thought. Saddling the pinto, he rode off.

Nathan was stocking shelves with quart canning jars. Rose was on the telephone. Ezra said, "I got some news about my Pa."

Setting down the box he was holding, Nathan asked, "Could it be from the man driving the car with Minnesota plates?"

Ezra grinned. "He stopped here for gasoline, didn't he?"

"He gassed up and left about an hour ago," Nathan said. "Now, what about Bert?"

"I want to get the whole Thorne family together and talk to them," Ezra said. "Can we meet here after church on Sunday?"

"Sure we can," Nathan said. "I will let Foley and Naomi know."

"I am going to ride over to Eban and Hannah's," Ezra said. "I've been planning to visit anyway."

"Is Bert still alive?" Nathan asked.

Ezra patted Nathan's shoulder. "I will tell you the whole story on Sunday."

After Sunday service, the general store held a party-like atmosphere. Hannah and Esther sliced warm bread while Naomi and Rose made ham and cheese sandwiches. Hannah had bought an apple pie and Naomi made her special chocolate cake. The men gathered around the table, waiting for Ezra.

"He only told me it was about Bertram," Nathan insisted. Ezra walked into the room, smiling.

"I'm glad you all could make it," he said. "I had a visit from Mr. Harlan DeWitt from New Ulm, Minnesota. In June of 1901, he rode west with Pa. Together, they made it to the Yukon." A chorus of "Oh, my gosh" and "I always wondered" floated around the room. When all had quieted down, Ezra continued. "I am going to tell you the whole story as Harlan told it to me." Reaching under his coat, Ezra took out the holster and revolver Harlan had given him and passed it around.

Nathan was the first to exclaim, "This is Bert's old Colt!" Eban and Foley nodded in agreement.

"The only way I can tell you this," Ezra said, "is to start at the beginning." And he did.

"Harlan told me he buried Pa on a hill behind their cabin on the Stuart River," Ezra concluded, "then he sold the claim and came home." There was a silence around the table as everyone waited for the facts to sink in.

Finally, Nathan said, "It sounds like your pa lived out his dream."

With a sigh, Ezra said, "Now I have something to tell you that will shock you all. When Harlan sold the claim, he got $25,000, plus Pa had $10,000 in the bank in Nome. Harlan gave me half, after taxes, of course." Taking out the little brown bank book, Ezra passed it around. "I have on deposit in the First National Bank of Burkesville, $19,500." The Thorne family was too stunned to respond; a quick gasp from Rose and a smile from Hannah said it all.

Nathan asked, "Have you been to the bank yet?"

"Not yet," Ezra replied, "but tomorrow, if Nathan will drive me, I plan to talk to some people about this."

Hannah had been watching Ezra, and with a smile, she said, "You already have a plan for this money, don't you, Ezra?"

Ezra nodded. "You know me all too well, Hannah. Yes, I have a plan."

Everyone at once asked, "What is the plan?" and "What will you do?"

"I have to talk to some people first," Ezra said, "but I think it will work out in the end. Gina always wanted to build a real children's wing in the hospital. All they have now is three rooms at the end of a hallway. This money could change that; at least, I hope so."

"What about something for yourself?" Rose asked.

Laughing, Ezra said, "I will finally get my bathroom!" The store rang with laughter, and the pie and cake were served.

Ezra's first stop on Monday morning was the bank. There were some papers to sign and questions to answer. Mr.

Franklin Edwards, the bank manager, asked if Ezra wanted a checking account or a savings account. "Savings account," Ezra said. "I just want to take out what I need when I need it."

"Do you need any cash now?" Franklin asked.

"I need $500," Ezra told him, "but I will be back later."

The next stop was the hospital. At the front desk, Ezra asked to see Doctor Nelson. "He is making his rounds," the nurse told him, "but you may wait in his office. It will be about 15 minutes."

When Dr. Nelson entered, Ezra and Nathan were sitting in the office talking about Bert.

"What can I do for you today?" he asked.

Smiling, Ezra said, "You need a children's wing built onto this hospital."

Taking off his glasses and rubbing the bridge of his nose, Dr. Nelson replied, "Ezra, we have been raising funds for a children's wing for three years. So far, we have collected $2200. The addition will cost us a total of $13,500. The money Gina left us helped, but we have a long way to go."

"I recently inherited some money," Ezra said. "Would you accept a donation of $12,000?"

Dr. Nelson stared at Ezra. "I don't know you well, Ezra, but well enough to believe you are serious. Do you really want to do this?"

Calmly, Ezra said, "I would like it to be called 'The Regina Forrest Children's Wing.'"

Still unable to believe this was happening, Dr. Nelson asked, "When will this money be available?"

Nathan, who had been watching all this, could not stop himself. "Let's go to the bank right now," he said.

"Good idea," Ezra said. "I will have the bank manager write you a check."

"Let me get my hat," the doctor said, "and I will meet you at the bank."

Franklin Edwards wrote out the check himself. "This is a wonderful thing you are doing," he told Ezra. "A great story for the newspaper."

Ezra shook his head. "No story, please. I prefer no one to know where this money came from. Can we agree on that?" Reluctantly, the doctor and the banker agreed.

"May I ask why?" said Dr. Nelson.

"I don't like everybody knowing my business," Ezra said. "It keeps the panhandlers away."

Everyone shook hands, and the doctor left, still smiling.

"Let's head home, Nathan," said Ezra.

The groundwork for the new wing began a week later. The newspaper made wild speculations on where the money to build came from, but the hospital and the bank stayed quiet. The plan for the new wing had been drafted a year ago, and all permits were issued and posted. The Thorne family all agreed to keep the story of Bertram Mulvey to themselves, with one exception, that being Conner Lundtz.

"I will tell Conner myself," Ezra said. "He has a right to know."

Conner took the news with a smile. "Bert found his place on earth in the Yukon. I'm just glad he left you and Micah here. Someday, Ezra, you and I should visit Arlington and visit Micah's grave."

"Someday, we will," Ezra replied.

Ezra hired Walt Tomlinson to build his bathroom. Nathan recommended Walt as he did good work at a reasonable price. "You can trust him," Nathan said.

Walt showed up one morning with a tape measure and a clipboard. "Show me where you want it," Walt said. Ezra wanted it attached to the rear of the cabin. Nodding his head, Walt took measurements and wrote on his clipboard. When he finished, he said, "My two sons, Fred and Lester, work with me. The job will take two weeks at a cost of $950. I need $300 now for materials."

Smiling, Ezra agreed.

CHAPTER TWENTY-TWO

Ezra sat on his bench watching Fred and Lester dig the trench for the water line from the well to the rear of the cabin. Two fluffy white clouds floated across the blue sky as the sun warmed the day. A car threw dust in the air as it turned into Ezra's yard.

As Sheriff Godfrey climbed out, he asked, "Is that all you have to do, watching men work?"

"Actually, no," Ezra said. "I plan on going fishing soon. Do you want to come along?"

"Not today," Luther said. "I got word this morning that a bank in Green Bay got robbed. The robbers are believed to be headed for Minneapolis, which means they might be headed this way. I need a few men for roadblocks if they decide to stop in Burkesville."

"You have my full attention," Ezra said. "I'll get my Colt and rifle and ride with you."

Eddie Boyce and Tony Dubeck met in a reform school in Racine when they were 15. Eddie was from Racine; Tony was from Milwaukee. Their first fight was with each other.

When it was over, they decided to be friends. When they were released at age 18, they decided to rob a grocery store. Eddie had a knife; Tony had a bat. The store owner had a .38 caliber pistol on the shelf below the register. Eddie got shot in the lower leg as he ran away.

Next, they tried a burglary, which netted them $12, a cheap watch, and an even cheaper .32 Iver Johnson pistol. Within a year, they had bungled themselves into a two-year jail sentence for a failed gas station holdup. Upon their release, they stole a car and drove to Fond du Lac. Both are now 21 and are as different as night and day. Eddie was 5 foot 10 inches tall, dark-complected, stocky, with dark brown hair. Tony was 6 feet tall, blonde hair, fair-skinned and slender. Eddie smoked Camels; Tony chewed gum.

Two burglaries in Fond du Lac got them gas money, a 20-gauge Remington pump shotgun, and a .38 Colt revolver. Then, they decided Green Bay was a nice town to visit and drove north.

"If we had some real money, we could go to Minneapolis," Eddie said. "I heard that the mayor there made a deal with the gangsters. If they left the town alone, the cops wouldn't arrest anybody."

"The banks got the big money," Tony said. "Let's check out some banks."

"The big banks got guards with guns," Eddie said. "A smaller bank should be easy."

At 9 o'clock, they robbed the Farmers & Merchants Bank. Nobody got hurt, and they got away with almost $4,000. Eddie drove as Tony counted the money. The bank manager called the city police, who called the Highway Patrol. Within

2 hours, every town in Wisconsin knew about the robbery, including Sheriff Luther Godfrey in Burkesville.

"If the robbers stay off the main highways, which they probably will," Luther speculated, "there is a good chance they might take 153, which goes right through Burkesville."

"A roadblock on both ends of town should do it," Ezra said.

"I only have two deputies available right now," Luther said. "I'll put you and one deputy on the east end, and I will take the west end with the rookie."

"What kind of auto are they driving?" Ezra asked.

"There is a barbershop next to the bank in Green Bay," Luther said, "the barber was looking out the window of his shop and saw two men run out of the bank. They got into a black Ford coupe and drove off. One was carrying a shotgun."

Eddie stopped for gas in Halder. A big woman in overalls filled their tank and washed the windshield. Tony paid her, and they drove on.

"We could have just driven away," Eddie said. "Why did you pay her?"

Smiling, Tony said, "She looked just like my Aunt Ruth, so I paid her."

Nodding his head, Eddie said, "I like this Ford, but I wish it had an 8-cylinder engine. Then we could outrun any patrol car."

"I'm getting hungry," Tony said. "Let's stop at the next diner." Eddie parked the Ford coupe in front of the Hilltop Diner outside Stratford. The only other vehicle there was an old Chevrolet truck with a few bales of straw in the bed. They sat at a table by the window so they could watch the traffic. The owner, a thin, bald man about 50, ambled over.

"What can I getcha?" he asked. Both men ordered cheeseburgers, home fries, and Coca-Cola's. Eddie lit a Camel while they waited for the food.

"How far to Minnesota?" he asked Tony.

"Couple hundred miles yet," Tony said. "We should be there by evening."

Ezra and the deputy stopped only one Ford coupe driven by a local attorney.

"Better take it home and park it," the deputy told him.

About noon, Ezra told the deputy, "Go to the diner and get us some food and drinks." The deputy got in the car and left. He was back in 20 minutes with hamburgers and drinks.

Eddie saw the deputy's car parked by the road half a mile away. "Looks like we got some law waiting for us," he said.

"Speed up and drive right at them," Tony said. "They will scatter like chickens."

Ezra saw the Ford coming and saw it speed up. "These must be our robbers," he yelled at the deputy. "Get down in the ditch!" Kneeling on the shoulder of the road, Ezra brought his Winchester up to his shoulder and squeezed off a shot.

BANG!

The driver's side front tire blew out, causing the speeding car to slide sideways.

BANG!

The rear tire was shredded. The Ford slammed over on its side and slid down into the right-hand ditch. The deputy's head poked up from the left-hand ditch, and he scrambled to his feet, pulling his revolver as he went.

Ezra walked over to the Ford just as Tony crawled out of the Ford window. He was dazed and bleeding from a cut to his cheek and holding the shotgun. Ezra pulled out his Colt, pointing it at Tony.

"Drop the gun," Ezra barked. Tony stared at Ezra for a moment, then dropped the shotgun. Eddie crawled out of the car window, wincing in pain.

"I think my leg is broken," he yelled.

Motioning to Tony, Ezra said, "Help him out of there and lay him on the grass."

Turning toward the deputy, Ezra said, "Go get Luther."

Pointing down the road, the deputy said, "Here he comes now."

Luther Godfrey slammed on his brakes and jumped out of his car. Down in the ditch, Tony had Eddie laid out on the grass. Tony felt the gun in Eddie's jacket pocket, reached in, and pulled it out. He pointed it at Ezra and yelled, "You god-damned hillbilly!"

Luther had seen the gun come up, drew his Colt double-action .38, and shot! The bullet broke Tony's shoulder, causing him to scream and drop his weapon. Ezra just stood for a moment, then grinned. "Thanks, Luther, nice shooting."

Luther turned a bit pale and was sweating. "Go get an ambulance," he told his deputy. Ezra went down and checked both men for any more weapons, then looked in the car. He saw the bag on the floorboard, picked it up, and looked inside.

"Bag full of money here, Luther," he said.

"Put it in my car," Luther told him. "We will take it back to the station and call Green Bay."

Ezra and a deputy followed the ambulance to the hospital. Two gurneys were waiting as the vehicle drove up. Tony and Eddie were loaded aboard and wheeled into the emergency room, where Doctor Nelson was waiting.

"Got to leave a deputy here," Ezra said. "These are the two bank robbers from Green Bay."

Dr. Nelson examined Tony first. "Bullet is lodged in the bone," he told the nurse. "Prep him for surgery." Eddie was next. "Lower left leg broken; get this one ready also." Turning to Ezra, Dr. Nelson smiled. "You always seem to be around when there is a gunshot wound."

With a smile, Ezra said, "Sheriff Godfrey shot that man and probably saved my life."

Dr. Nelson patted Ezra's shoulder, saying, "An angel is watching over you, and we both know who it is."

Nodding his head, Ezra said softly, "Her body is gone, Doc, but her spirit is here with me every day."

At the sheriff's station, Ezra told Luther, "I left the rookie deputy at the hospital to guard the prisoners."

"The deputy on vacation is due tomorrow," Luther said, "so you can go home anytime."

Grinning, Ezra said, "I rode in here with you, so I need a ride home."

Nodding his head, Luther said, "Alright, but pour us a cup of coffee first." As Ezra poured, Luther said, "In all my years in law enforcement, today was the first time I ever shot anybody."

"I suspected as much," Ezra said. "It ain't a good feeling, but sometimes it's necessary. You probably saved my life."

Luther was quiet for a moment. "You were there because I needed your experience, and I trusted you to do the job, and you didn't let me down. When I saw that gun come up in that robber's hand, I knew I couldn't let you down. Simple as that."

Grinning, Ezra said, "That's why I voted for you, Luther."

CHAPTER TWENTY-THREE

"I just took something in trade that is perfect for you," Nathan said as he exited the storeroom. Ezra had stopped to check his mail and buy some coffee.

"Ain't got time," Ezra said, "got to cut some hay today."

Nathan laughed and said, "That's what I want to show you! It's a McCormick-Deering horse-drawn mower! You harness your horse to it, and it does all the work!"

The idea appealed to Ezra, who still cut hay with a scythe. "Let's take a look." Next to the barn, behind the store, were several pieces of farm equipment. The mower looked in good condition. "You sure it works?" Ezra asked.

"I had Foley check it over and run it," Nathan said. "He told me this machine is in very good condition."

"Show me how it works," Ezra said.

Nathan made his living as a salesman, and it was not wasted on Ezra. Sitting on the metal seat, Nathan went through the operation, raising and lowering the sickle bar with ease. Then Ezra tried it. Within minutes, he was sold.

"What does it cost, and when can you bring it over?"

"For you, it is $50, and I can deliver it this morning."

Smiling, Ezra stuck out his hand. "You got a deal."

At the cabin, the Tomlinson's were cutting a hole in the back wall of the cabin where the door to the bathroom would be. The bathroom floor was in, with pipes sticking through.

"How are you going to do the roof?" Ezra asked.

Walt pointed and said, "It will be just like the roof you have now, only a few feet lower."

"Good idea," Ezra said. "By the way, I'll be cutting hay in my back pasture if you need me."

What used to take Ezra two days, and then some, took one afternoon. When he finished, he sat on the mower and looked over the field. Smiling, he thought, 'Ain't this grand. Still got time to do some fishing.'

He drove back to the barn and parked the mower. Removing the harness from his brown horse, he turned it into the corral and saddled the pinto. He had his favorite spot on Otter Lake and was there in less than half an hour.

Digging in the ground with his knife, Ezra unearthed several red worms. Threading two on the hook, he tossed the line in the water. In less than fifteen minutes, he caught three fat sunfish. As he dug more worms, he heard tree branches moving and footsteps. Looking around, he saw a man he had not seen in years.

"Glad to see you back, Tom White Elk," he said with a smile. "We were boys when you left the Crossroads."

The Menominee Indian had grown to almost six feet. "I remember you, Ezra Mulvey," he said. "Good hunter, good friend." Tom was leading a pack horse, upon which sat a slender woman.

"You have a wife now," Ezra said.

"Her name is Bluebird," Tom said. "We are going to the reservation at Shawano to live."

"You have a long journey," Ezra said. "I have another fishline. You fish with me, and we will have a fish fry at my cabin, where you will spend the night."

Within an hour, the two men had a dozen fish: a mix of sunfish, bluegills, and perch.

Back at the cabin, the builders had quit for the day. "You building an addition on your place?"

"Adding a bathroom," Ezra explained. "Much warmer in the winter than the outhouse."

Laughing, Tom said, "And a hot bath never hurts."

"I have potatoes and onions to go with the fish," Ezra said. "Bluebird can find all she needs in the cabin while you and I clean the fish."

Noticing the fire pit, Bluebird said, "I will cook outside. Food tastes better over fire."

As they ate, Ezra asked, "Where have you been all these years?"

"Mostly traveling," Tom said, "worked on some farms, then caught on with some grain harvesters. We worked in Iowa, Kansas, Minnesota, and as far south as Missouri. When winter came, I went west to Colorado, but it was winter there too, so I washed dishes in a cafe until spring, then back to the harvest circuit."

Ezra sipped his coffee. "What made you come back here?"

Pointing at Bluebird, Tom said, "About two years ago,

I met Bluebird. She was cooking for a family in Nebraska, where we harvested oats. She told me her family lived on the reservation. She left there with a boy who was a rodeo rider. That boy got killed when a horse threw him, and he broke his back. We are both Menominee, so we got married and worked our way back here."

"What will you do on the reservation?" Ezra asked.

Smiling, Tom said, "I can always find work."

Bluebird was gathering up the dishes. "I will wash these, then we will sleep in the loft on the hay," she said. "Better than a hard floor."

The following day, Tom helped Ezra turn the cut hay into windrows to dry it. Bluebird packed their things, anxious to be on her way.

"She worries about her folks getting old," Tom said. "They have a small farm, just three cows, some pigs, and chickens. I will probably be working for them."

"It was really good to visit with you again," Ezra said. "I wish Micah were here, but the war took him. I just recently found out my pa died in the Yukon looking for gold."

"Your pa was always looking for something," Tom said. "He must have found it." The two men shook hands. Bluebird climbed on the horse, and they left, headed for Shawano.

The first hay crop was in the loft, the garden was planted, and the new bathroom was almost done. The sink and toilet were installed, and the bathtub would arrive today. Ezra was saddling the pinto when the Tomlinson's truck drove in.

Walt Tomlinson got out and waved at Ezra. "Got your bathtub here. We could use a bit of help unloading it." Tom's sons, Fred and Lester, were on the truck, untying the ropes holding the tub. "Ezra, you take one side, and I will take the other."

Slowly, the tub was inched out over the edge. As it tipped down, the two men eased it to the ground. "We can take it from here," Walt said.

"I will be gone till this afternoon," Ezra said as he mounted his horse. "Got some personal business to tend to."

"If everything goes well," Walt said, "we should finish up today."

Gray clouds were forming in the northwest. 'Maybe have rain tonight,' Ezra thought. He stopped briefly to check a wild raspberry patch he picked from every year. It was flourishing, the new growth swaying in the light breeze. Rabbits darted through the underbrush.

'Should have brought some snares,' he thought. Soon, Ezra emerged from the woods and entered the opening of Gina's Valley. He dismounted, unsaddled, and staked the pinto out to graze. The entire valley floor was awash with color. The flowers moved ever so gently in the breeze. The creek below tumbled over the rocks with the occasional splash of a fish. The birch trees on the other shore were like a white picket fence of leaves and branches.

Ezra bent down to admire the rose bush he had planted over Gina's ashes. It was blooming bright red, as if in enjoyment of living.

"It's me, Gina," Ezra said softly. "It seems the winter treated you well. I have been well. It has been an eventful time, and I am here to share with you."

Ezra told Gina all that had happened as he sipped from his canteen and lunched on biscuits and bacon. As he glanced over the valley, a Cardinal lit on the lower branch of the oak tree. It cocked its head from time to time as if listening to Ezra's conversation.

He had brought an extra canteen of water and slowly watered the rose bush. Then it was time to leave.

"I will be back before fall," he promised. He saddled up, mounted, and rode home.

It was late afternoon by the time Ezra got home. Dismounting, he saw all three Tomlinson's sitting on the porch, each with a bottle of root beer. Walt reached behind him and pulled out another bottle. "Join us," he said. "We always have one after we finish a job."

"Let me unsaddle, and I'll join you," Ezra said with a smile. Five minutes later, he was back, took the bottle, and sat down.

"Got some rain coming," Walt said. "Looks like we finished just in time."

"Run into any problems?" Ezra asked.

"Not a one," Walt answered. "Everything went together just as it should. C'mon. Let's do a final inspection." The two men rose and entered the cabin. Opening the door to the bathroom, Walt said, "Try all the taps."

Ezra smiled as water ran freely from the sink and the tub. When he pulled the chain for the toilet, he watched as the water flushed out.

Pointing up, Walt said, "The window is a double pane, keeps it warmer in here but will open also." Then he pointed to the floor. "We used all hardwood. During the winter, push some burlap bags filled with straw underneath to insulate the pipes."

"Is all this guaranteed not to leak?" Ezra asked.

Nodding his head, Walt said, "If you have any leak in the first year, you call me, and I will fix it, no charge."

In the cabin, Ezra went to the chest at the foot of his bed and took out a wooden box. He opened it and removed an envelope. Handing it to Walt, he said, "Your payment."

Without opening the envelope, Walt stuck it in his pocket and pulled out his wallet. From it, he took a sheet of paper. It was a list of materials, their cost, and time worked. He signed his name, wrote 'paid in full,' and gave it to Ezra. The two men shook hands and went back outside, where the Tomlinson's got in their truck and drove away.

Looking around, Ezra spotted his next project. 'Tomorrow, I burn down the outhouse and fill in the hole,' he thought with a grin.

The snares Ezra put out for rabbits yielded four that morning. Without them, his garden would be ravaged. He kept one for his supper. 'These would be a good trade for some fresh-baked bread,' he thought.

Saddling up, he headed for Eban and Hannah Thorne's farm. Their land adjoined along a slow-moving, no-name creek. He stopped when he noticed a paw print in the mud on the creek bank. Dismounting, Ezra examined it further. 'Bobcat,' he thought, 'not too big, maybe a young male.' Mounting, he continued on.

Cresting the top of a low hill, he rode down the path

along the woodlot until he reached the farm. Eban was watering his team of harnessed Belgian horses at the trough. Noticing the three rabbits hanging from Ezra's saddle horn, he smiled and said, "I bet I know what we are having for supper."

"How much hay do you have to bring in yet?" Ezra asked.

"Two more loads should do it," Eban said. "I have an extra pitchfork if you remember how to use one."

"I'll give Hannah these rabbits and be right back," Ezra said.

Hannah had seen him arrive and was waiting on the porch. Ezra handed her the furry bundle.

"Thank you, Ezra," she said. "Will you join us for supper?"

"Thank you, but no, Hannah," he said. "I have one of those waiting for me at the cabin. I am out of bread, though."

"Esther and I are baking today," Hannah said. "I will have a loaf ready for you."

Eban's son, Daniel, now almost eight years old, drove the team as Ezra and Eban spread the hay around the wagon as it cascaded off the hay loader. The men packed the hay down with their feet as best they could. When he felt the load of hay was full, Eban hollered, "Whoa!"

Ezra slid down the hay and unhooked the hay-loader. "Take it to the barn," he told Daniel. Daniel halted the team at the barn under the hay hook suspended from an overhead beam. Ezra went into the barn and climbed the ladder to the mow as Daniel unhitched the horses from the wagon and backed them alongside.

A long rope hung from the hay-hook, which Daniel

hooked to the team's singletree. Atop the wagon, Eban lowered the hook with his rope and stomped the four long prongs deep into the hay.

"Pull!" Eban yelled. Slowly, Daniel led the team forward until the hook reached the top of the beam. A loud metal 'click,' and the hook was set. Inside the mow, Ezra pulled the load of hay in until it was where he wanted it, then tripped the hook, which spilled the load of hay.

"Go!" yelled Ezra, and Eban pulled the empty hook out to the end of the beam, lowered it, and repeated the process. Each knew their job and did it well.

"Nathan says you finally bought a mower," Eban said as the two men sipped iced tea on the front porch after the hay was in.

Smiling, Ezra said, "Yes, and I should have got one years ago."

"Let me know when your second crop is ready, and I will bring the hay-loader over."

"Thank you, Daniel," Ezra said as the boy led his saddled horse to the porch. As he mounted, Hannah came out and handed Ezra a wrapped loaf of bread.

"Now, don't be such a stranger," she said with a smile. The bread went in the saddlebag, then Ezra tipped his hat, turned the horse, and rode up the lane.

CHAPTER TWENTY-FOUR

Lucas and June Hatch lived six miles from the Crossroads. No one knew exactly how many children they had, but two of them, Vernell and Dexter, were always in trouble, mostly of their own making. Vernell, the oldest, was 18. At five foot ten, he was scrawny, with brown hair and a ragged beard. Dexter was 16, five foot eight, pudgy, with dark hair. Some younger children were enrolled in the school because the county demanded it.

What Lucas Hatch did for a living was a mystery. The family received aid from the county through food and donated clothing. To get around, Lucas Hatch owned an old, gray-muzzled mule that could barely pull the old spring wagon. The family did not attend the church or shop at the Crossroads store. How the family made it through the winters was anyone's guess, but they did. The Ladies Aid Society visited once to offer help.

"We don't need church women telling us how to live," Lucas yelled as he waved them away. The ladies left and did not return.

"It's those Hatch boys again," Sheriff Godfrey muttered, sipping his coffee on the bench outside Ezra's cabin.

"What did they do now?"

"They broke into Joe Melinski's hen house," Luther said. "Joe caught them trying to leave with four chickens. He held them at gunpoint against the barn while his wife drove to town for a deputy."

"You got them in jail," Ezra said, "so what is your problem?"

Sipping coffee, Luther said, "They went before the judge yesterday, and he gave them each a $30 fine or 30 days in jail."

Smiling, Ezra said, "I guess you don't want them lying around the jail eating free food and sleeping all day."

Laughing, Luther said, "The fact is, I've already got Dexter working with the crew building that new wing of the hospital. Without Vernell around, he will behave himself. I've got other plans for Vernell."

"Doing what?" Ezra asked.

"Got a lot of gravel roads in the county that have potholes that need filling," Luther said, "but I can't leave him alone. He would be gone in a flash."

"So you want me to ride herd on him," Ezra said.

"My deputies have more important work that needs doing, and the county will pay you $5 a day."

Ezra paused. "I've got work to do also, Luther, but here is what I will do. I will do the first week and the third week. A deputy can do the second and fourth week."

Luther removed his hat, scratched his head, put the hat back on, and said, "I'll have a truck loaded with gravel on the road a mile from the bridge on Monday morning. Vernell will be in the truck with the driver. The county will pack him a sack lunch."

Monday morning dawned cloudy and cool. Ezra was waiting on horseback when the county truck drove up. "I'm gonna turn around so the prisoner can shovel gravel off the back," the driver told him. "Then I back over it and pack it down."

Vernell got out of the truck and stared at Ezra. "What are you doing here, Mulvey?"

Grinning, Ezra said, "I'm hoping you try to run so I can chase you; now get up in the truck bed and start shoveling."

They stopped at noon, having covered about six miles. Ezra had brought food and water. He sat in the shade of an elm tree, watching Vernell.

The man's hair and clothing were covered in gravel dust as he sat on the ground, his back against the rear truck tire.

"I don't like you staring at me, Mulvey," he growled.

"Why were you stealing chickens, Vernell?"

"Me and Dex were hungry," Vernell muttered.

"Most people work to buy food when they get hungry," Ezra said. "Only lazy trash steal their food."

Sensing a fight coming on, the truck driver intervened. "Lunch is over; let's get back to work."

Vernell picked up his shovel and stood up. Ezra stood with his back to Vernell. Taking one step forward, Ezra immediately dropped to one knee as he heard the SWOOSH! of the shovel as it passed over his head.

Rising, Ezra turned, smiling. He kicked Vernell in the shin, hard. With a choked scream, Vernell dropped the shovel and bent over to grab his leg. As he did, Ezra's knee came up to meet Vernell's chin. Without a sound, Vernell flew backward and lay spread-eagled on the ground, out cold.

The driver just stood by the truck, his eyes wide, staring. He finally managed to say, "He tried to kill you with that shovel!"

Ezra winked at the driver. "Trying don't always get it done," he said. Taking the jug of water from the truck, Ezra slowly poured some over Vernell's face. Slowly, Vernell came to, shaking his head.

"Got a lot more potholes to fill this afternoon," Ezra said. "Better get to it."

Dragging himself to his feet, Vernell limped to the truck and climbed up. Ezra picked up the shovel and tossed it onto the pile of gravel. Vernell picked it up and looked at it a moment, then went back to work.

The rest of the week was pretty quiet. Vernell did his job, and Ezra left him alone. By Friday, Vernell's limp was gone. The truck driver told everyone he ran into about the shovel incident. Most people just nodded or shook their heads. The most repeated comment was, "That Hatch boy got off easy."

Sheriff Godfrey had Dr. Nelson check Vernell's shin. "Just a bruise," the doctor said. "Didn't even break the skin." The following week, the deputy in charge had no problem until Friday. It was a hot day, and the deputy and the driver fell asleep in the truck during lunch break. When they awoke, Vernell was long gone.

Sheriff Godfrey drove slowly into Ezra's yard Saturday just after noon. Ezra was working in his garden, harvesting a bumper crop of tomatoes. "I know your wife cans tomatoes," Ezra said, "so you take some of these with you."

"Thanks, I will," Luther said. "I came to tell you that my deputy fell asleep on the job Friday, and Vernell ran off. He could be in Minnesota by now."

Ezra shook his head. "Right now, he is hiding in the big swamp waiting for Dexter to be released. Then they will leave together."

The sheriff frowned and asked, "How do you figure that?"

Walking to his cabin, Ezra said, "Let's have some iced tea, and I will explain Vernell to you."

Sitting in the shade of the cabin, Ezra sipped iced tea. "Vernell Hatch is a petty thief and a coward. Every time he gets into trouble, Dexter is with him. Vernell is afraid to be on his own because he feels powerless. He needs someone to back him up, and Dexter is the only one he can trust."

Luther nodded his head. "That makes sense, but how do we get Vernell back?"

Grinning, Ezra said, "That's the easy part, Luther. Let Dexter serve one more week, then give him a week off for good behavior. He will head right for the swamp to get Vernell, and when they come out, we take them."

"That's a big swamp," Luther said. "Vernell could be hiding anywhere."

"We don't go in at night," Ezra said. "All your deputies would get lost. We wait and arrest them out on the road, off their property."

"You plan to be there?" Luther asked.

"Wouldn't miss it," Ezra said with a big smile.

"Now you go home and behave yourself," Sheriff Godfrey told Dexter. "I don't want to see you back here for at least a year." Dexter walked out to the edge of town and, within an hour, caught a ride with the gasoline truck going to the Crossroads. He thanked the driver and walked up the road toward home. It was mid-afternoon on Friday, and Dexter was in no big hurry. Every once in a while, he would look behind him, but the road was empty. June Hatch was hanging out the wash when Dexter ambled down the drive.

"Hot coffee on the stove," she said. "Your pa is sleeping, don't wake him."

"Vernell around?" Dexter asked. "Went back in the swamp after breakfast," June said. "They let you out early?"

"Time off for good behavior," Dexter said.

"I guess miracles do happen," June muttered.

At dusk, two patrol cars parked in front of the store. Sheriff Godfrey and a young deputy got out of one car, the senior deputy, Glen Townley, and another deputy from the other. Ezra was already there, his horse hitched to the railing.

"You know that area, Ezra," the sheriff said. "What do you want us to do?"

"I've trapped the swamp," Ezra said, "and to go in, I use a game trail about a mile north of Hatch's place. It's the only way to get in and out without getting bogged down. If I know it, so does Vernell."

"How do we set up?" Luther asked.

"We use both cars, a half mile apart, with the trail in the middle. There is only a quarter moon tonight, so they won't see you. When they come out on the road, turn on your headlights, drive toward them, and tell them to lay down on the road."

"What if they turn around and head back up the trail?" asked Glen Townley.

Smiling, Ezra said, "I'll be behind them when they come out. Remember, we don't want Dexter, just Vernell."

Ezra found a spot in the tall grass and weeds and waited. An owl hooted, an eerie sound in the darkness. Then, he saw the pale glow from a lantern and muffled voices coming up the trail. Ezra dropped to one knee and waited.

"Slow down, Dex," Vernell said in a low tone. "We ain't in no hurry."

"We are almost to the road," Dexter said. "Then we can go home." As the two men stepped out onto the dirt road, the patrol cars turned on their headlights, catching them completely off guard. Dexter, still holding the lantern, stood with his mouth open.

"Lay down on the road, now!" yelled Sheriff Godfrey as the cars stopped just a few yards away. Dexter set his lantern down and lay down; Vernell turned and bolted back up the trail, running head-first into Ezra. With a shove, Vernell was pushed backward, lost his balance, and sat down heavily on the road. He looked up into the smiling face of Ezra Mulvey.

"Turn over so the deputy can cuff you," Ezra said. Knowing he was caught, Vernell slowly turned on his stomach and put his hands behind his back. Deputy Townley cuffed Vernell's hands, stood him up, and put the prisoner in the patrol car.

The sheriff patted Dexter on the shoulder. "You can go home now," Luther told him. "And thanks for your help in apprehending this fugitive." Dexter slowly shook his head, picked up his lantern, and walked toward home.

CHAPTER TWENTY-FIVE

Sawing logs into firewood was not Ezra's favorite chore, but it needed to be done. It was mid-morning when Eban Thorne drove into the yard.

"Thought you would be cutting that last crop of hay," Ezra said.

Eban got out of his Ford and said, "Something tried to kill one of my heifers last night. The heifer got away, but I had to call the vet to patch it up."

Ezra laid down his saw. "Go on home, Eban. I'll get cleaned up and be there in an hour." As Eban left, Ezra picked up his shirt and entered the cabin. He washed, buckled on his Colt revolver, picked up his rifle, and went to saddle his horse.

Taking the trail to the Thorne farm, Ezra crossed the creek into the upper meadow. He found the place the heifer had been attacked. Streaks of blood lay over the grass. While trying to escape, the heifer's hooves had torn up the grass, leaving a spot of bare earth with a print in the middle. Dismounting, Ezra studied the print closely. Thumbing back his hat, he muttered, "I'll be damned, a cougar!" Mounting, Ezra hurried to the farm.

Hannah poured coffee for Ezra and Eban on the front porch. "Are you sure it's a cougar?" Eban asked. "There hasn't been one around for over 20 years."

"Years ago, my pa killed a cougar while trapping in Rusk County," Ezra said. "I was just a boy, but I remember him bringing that beast home. Pa said it was just beginning to get light out, and he was set to shoot a deer drinking at a creek. Suddenly, this cougar comes out of nowhere and leaps on the deer. Pa shot and killed it, then shot the deer. While Pa was skinning out that cat, I picked up one of those big paws and looked it over. I will never forget it. That cougar pelt brought in more money than all his other pelts."

"What would a cougar be doing in this part of the state?" Eban asked.

"The state is growing," Ezra said. "Loggers cutting hardwoods up north, farmers expanding their fields, towns growing into cities—all this is pushing animals out of their natural hunting grounds. Let's hope he doesn't have a mate."

"How do you plan to get this cougar?" Hannah asked Ezra as she stepped onto the porch.

"I have an idea I think will work," Ezra said, "but it will take two men."

"If it will save some livestock, count me in," Eban said.

"First, I have to find out where it is holed up. I have a general idea where it might be, but I need to do some tracking and planning."

Late that afternoon, Ezra found what he was looking for.

It was on the outer northern edge of his property, bordering state forest land. A short range of hills and sandstone outcroppings, seldom used by anyone, yielded natural erosion that had given way to some shallow caves.

Suddenly, his horse had grown uneasy, snorting and backing up, not wanting to go further. Ezra dismounted, tied the horse, and searched for tracks. He found one in a sandy patch of ground. Mounting, he rode slowly in a spreading half-circle, moving outward.

About a quarter mile away, he located a huge elm tree that had blown down, landing on its big limbs. The size of the elm had driven the limbs into the earth, leaving the elm at an angle about fifteen feet off the ground. Ezra climbed up until he found a spot that gave him the height he wanted. 'This should do nicely,' he thought and climbed down. His horse had calmed down and was browsing on some tall grass. Ezra mounted and rode home.

"I don't see how I'm helping you sitting a half mile away," Eban said.

Smiling, Ezra said, "Just knowing you and the horses are here eases my mind." The two men were in a small clearing ringed by birch and maple trees. Ezra had two dead rabbits hanging from his saddle horn. Both men carried Winchester rifles.

"I don't want the horses any closer," Ezra said. "That cougar will smell them and shy away. I need total quiet to concentrate on any movement."

"How long do you think it will be?"

"Hard to tell. I'm hoping an hour or so, but when you

hear me shoot, you ride in." Ezra handed the reins to Eban as he dismounted, unhooked the rabbits, and walked away.

Ezra stopped by a small maple tree about 25 yards from the toppled elm. Ensuring he had a clear line of sight, he hung the rabbits from a branch at shoulder height. Slowly, he approached the elm and climbed up. When he found the right spot, he stopped and leaned against an upright branch. It was a warm day with few clouds. The trees around Ezra offered some shade and helped conceal his form.

'Now we wait,' he thought, 'and I hope that cat is hungry.'

The day dragged on. A woodpecker off to his left began working on an old stump. Squirrels dashed through the leaves and tall grass. Ezra never moved, as still as one of the trees around him, listening for movement on the ground, watching for any sign of the cougar. The sun slowly moved toward the horizon, and a slight breeze moved the leaves of the trees. Then he saw it!

Just a tawny splash of color moving slowly through the grass. It stopped, then moved again, coming closer to the smell of the two rabbits. Then it was in the open, sniffing the air. A low growl came from its throat as the big head lifted toward the hanging bait.

BANG!

BANG!

The two shots were so close together that they sounded like one. The cougar dropped to the ground, twitched its hind legs once, and went still. Ezra waited a few minutes before climbing down from his perch. He slowly approached the still form, his rifle at the ready. Then he relaxed, smiling. Two bullet holes could be seen an inch apart through the cougar's head.

Ezra was examining the cougar when Eban rode up. "That was the longest afternoon of my life," Eban said. He dismounted and moved the horses back until they quieted down. Ezra was examining the teeth and claws of the big cat.

"This is an old timer," Ezra said. "The teeth are blunt, and one has a broken tip. The claws are worn down, and there is some scarring on one of the hind pads like he might have stepped in a trap years ago."

Looking close, Eban asked, "Why shoot him in the head?"

"Didn't want to spoil the pelt."

"Now what do we do?" Eban asked.

"Now we hang him up, gut him, and peel the hide off," Ezra said.

It was almost dark when they got back to Ezra's cabin. Eban mumbled something about "got cows to milk." Then he got in his Ford and drove away. Lighting a lantern, Ezra set it on a wood block and got to work. He pegged the cougar's hide to the outside wall of the cabin. He rubbed it down well with salt twice. Standing back, he lifted the lantern high and admired the pelt.

'Should bring a good price,' he thought. It would take time for the hide to cure. 'Back to sawing logs tomorrow,' he thought. 'A man's work is never done.'

Ezra was splitting and stacking the wood next to the cabin. Gray clouds were forming to the northwest, promising rain soon. Eban's Ford drove into the yard, and he had brought the family with him. Hannah got out of the car and held out a napkin-covered dish.

"Esther and I baked pies yesterday," she said with a smile, "and I know you like apple."

Ezra took the dish. "I thank you most kindly; apple is my favorite."

Stepping forward, Esther said shyly, "I made the crust; I hope you like it."

"Soon, you will be baking rings around your mother." Esther smiled, blushed, and giggled all at once. The boys—Daniel, Jacob, and young Noah—were admiring the cougar pelt.

"It's really big," Daniel said.

"It smells salty," Jacob said, wrinkling his nose.

"Takes a lot of salt to cure a hide that big," Ezra told him.

Noah just stared at the pelt.

"How is the heifer doing?" Ezra asked Eban.

"Took a lot of stitches. Kept the vet busy all morning."

"What Nathan can get for the pelt should cover the vet bill, with some leftover," Ezra said.

"You sure you want to do that?" Eban asked.

"You helped get this pelt; you share in the profit."

Hannah leaned forward and kissed Ezra on the cheek. "Thank you. From all of us."

Ezra, finally at a loss for words, smiled and blushed. Hannah clapped her hands and said, "Back in the car, boys, it's time to go home." As they drove away, Ezra smiled, touched his cheek, and nodded. Sighing, he muttered, "women."

CHAPTER TWENTY-SIX

"Did Doctor Nelson say why he wanted to talk to me?" Ezra asked Nathan. They were in Nathan's Dodge driving into Burkesville.

"He didn't really give me a reason. He just told me it was important."

Ezra had taken time to shave and put on a clean shirt.

"Did you leave your revolver at home?" Nathan asked with a grin.

Laughing, Ezra said, "I feel naked without it, but yes, I left it at home."

"When will that cougar pelt be ready?" Nathan asked. "I've got a buyer lined up for it."

Ezra rubbed his chin. "I'll bring it in next week." As they entered the town, he said, "I should stop at the bank today and check on my account."

"Still don't trust the banks?" Nathan asked.

"Sure I do," Ezra said, "but it doesn't hurt to check on them now and then."

Dr. Nelson was waiting for them in his office. He had blueprints of the new children's wing spread across his desk.

"The reason I asked you to be here today, Ezra, is to show you the plan and explain the reasons for the way it is laid out."

"From what I have seen outside, the work is going fine," Ezra said.

"Let me show you what will be available for the children. It will be the finest facility in the state." The doctor pointed out a waiting room, an examination room, an X-ray lab, a surgery room, and another doctor's office. "More donations have been coming in, thanks to your generous gift."

Pointing at the new doctor's office, Ezra asked, "Are you getting another doctor?"

A smile spread across Dr. Nelson's face. "We can hire a doctor specializing in children's care and two more nurses. Gina would be so happy to see the children well cared for."

"You know she is watching over us as we speak," Ezra said with a smile.

Swiftly wiping away the tear in his eye, Dr. Nelson said softly, "I feel her presence every day."

Ezra and Nathan left the hospital and went to the bank. The manager, Mr. Edwards, saw them enter and came out of his office. "Good morning, Mr. Thorne and Mr. Mulvey. How may I help you?"

"I need to draw out some money," Ezra said. "$200 should do it."

"Certainly," Mr. Edwards said. "If you will have a seat, I will have my secretary do that right now." In less than five minutes, the two men were on their way.

"Where to next?"

"The vet's office," Ezra said. "I want to take care of the bill for Eban's heifer."

"I thought the money from selling the cougar pelt would take care of that," Nathan said.

Smiling, Ezra said, "No reason to make the vet wait, and this way, Eban doesn't get a bill."

"The bill is $50," the secretary behind the counter said. Ezra handed her the money and got a copy of the bill marked 'paid.'

Nathan scratched his head. "I don't know if that pelt will bring that much."

"If it does, that's fine," Ezra said. "If not, no matter – and only you and I will know."

"Which means I can't tell Rose," Nathan said. The two were laughing when they left.

The cougar pelt brought $45 from the buyer. While inspecting it, he frowned. "I can't find the bullet holes," he said.

"That's because I shot it in the head," Ezra told him.

"You must be one hell of a shot," the buyer said with a grin.

Looking the man in the eyes, Ezra replied, "Yep."

The man's grin vanished; he paid the money, took the pelt, and left.

Good weather held for the harvest. Ezra made his third cutting of hay in one afternoon. He would have more than enough to last the winter. As promised, Eban showed up with a wagon and hayloader. Daniel was with him and would drive the tractor. Ezra had turned the hay into windrows the day before, a slow job done by hand but necessary. By late afternoon, the last load was in the mow.

As they sat on the bench by the cabin, Ezra said, "Daniel, there are some cold bottles of root beer in a bucket of water in the cabin. Would you get us one?"

As they sipped the drink, Eban said, "Hannah would like you to have Sunday dinner with us."

"Count me in," Ezra said. "What are we having?"

"Herman Kruetzer brought over a smoked ham, and we have some new red potatoes to go with it."

Snapping his fingers, Ezra said, "That reminds me, I have a pie dish I need to give back. I will bring it along, and tell Esther the pie crust was delicious."

Smiling, Eban said, "I will tell her. See you Sunday."

As Eban and Daniel drove away, Ezra thought, "They truly are our family, Gina.'

"Didn't I hear you bought a Farmall tractor?" Foley asked old Carl. Carl Erlinger had bought his team of Clydesdales in to be shod.

"I sure did," Carl said, "and it does a fine job. Then again, there is work only a horse can do." Many of the local farmers felt the same. They had begun farming with horses, just as their fathers had. The horse was family. A team of horses was still a mainstay on almost every farm in the county. "There are places on my farm where I cannot and would not take a tractor," Carl said.

"How old are these two horses?" Foley asked.

Rubbing his chin a moment, Carl said, "I bought them

as a pair just before the big war, so they would be about fifteen years old."

"The price of horseshoes has gone up," Foley told him. "It's 50 cents a shoe more."

"No matter. I'll be in the store getting some supplies."

Foley pointed up to the big bell hanging by the forge door. "When they are ready, I will ring the bell."

"Just go ahead and move," Carl said. "You play like an old woman who can't make up her mind." It was the second game of checkers with Rufus Dawes.

"You just settle down, old man," Rufus said. "I'll move when I'm good and ready." The little bell above the door chimed as Ezra entered the store.

"Howdy Ezra," Carl said. "Heard you been out hunting cougar."

"Not just hunting, but killing," Rufus added.

"Had to do it," Ezra replied. "It almost got one of Eban's heifers."

"Where do you suppose it came from?" Carl asked.

"Maybe up around the Iron River country," Rufus said, "or maybe came down from Canada."

"Maybe," Ezra said. "Hope we don't get any more."

BONG!

BONG!

"Foley must be done shoeing my team," Carl said. "Make your move so I can go home, Rufus."

Rufus moved a red checker.

"Gotcha," Carl said. His black checker jumped three of the reds. "You keep practicing, Rufus. I'll be back in a month to beat you again."

Nathan came in from outside. He was dusty and smudged with dirt.

Grinning, Ezra said, "Looks like you been wrestling with someone or something."

"Going to have a sale," Nathan said. "I'm getting rid of all that old farm machinery by the barn."

"Let's go take a look," Ezra said. "You might have something I can use."

As they walked out, Nathan asked, "Got your last hay in?"

Ezra nodded. "Eban brought his hay loader over; got it done in one afternoon."

In front of the barn, Nathan had lined up the equipment. Much of it was outdated but still usable. One item caught Ezra's eye. A light spring wagon made to be pulled by one horse. "I like this wagon," Ezra said as he looked it over. "I could haul my squash, potatoes, carrots, and red onions in one trip from the garden to the cabin."

"Twenty dollars," Nathan said, "and I'll deliver it this evening." They smiled as they shook hands on the deal.

The weather had been perfect for gardens this year, with plenty of sunshine and rain when needed. Ezra had been giving away tomatoes to anyone who would take them. The wagon he had bought from Nathan was parked at the end of the garden. Having tried a few different varieties of squash, Ezra settled on the acorn and butternut squash. For two reasons. They were durable and would last through the winter with no spoilage. Also, Ezra liked their nutty flavor. Roasted in the oven, then served with butter and a little salt.

The big red onions were great for stew or cooked with a thick venison steak; maybe add a few mushrooms. Carrots were mainly for stews and sometimes just for a snack. The russet potato was all Ezra had ever grown. It went in stews, baked in the oven, fried with bacon and eggs, and could be a meal in itself. Stored properly, these vegetables would see Ezra through the winter. Venison, grouse, and rabbit were taken as needed.

Hannah Thorne and most of the other Crossroads women canned venison every fall. Ezra smiled as he loaded the wagon. 'Should take Hannah some squash and carrots,' he thought. 'Chance to show off my new wagon.'

"Well, aren't you the proper country gentleman," Hannah said with a smile, "traveling around in a wagon now."

"It's the only way to deliver an abundance of squash and carrots," Ezra said with a grin. Hannah looked in the wagon. "We can certainly use both. Those men of mine love their squash."

"Is Eban around?"

"Eban took Esther and Daniel berry picking," Hannah said, "and tomorrow Esther and I will be making jam and pies."

"That reminds me, I have some berries of my own to bring in," Ezra said.

"When you have them picked," Hannah said, "bring them here, and we will preserve them for you."

"You throw in a pie, and I will do just that."

Ezra stopped at the store on his way home. Rose was

behind the counter as he walked in. "Just got in some new wool shirts and socks," she said.

"Could use some new socks," Ezra said, "and a pair of long johns."

"A letter came for you yesterday," Rose said. "I will get it while you look around." Rose was back in a moment waving a letter.

"It's from a law office in Minnesota." He opened the envelope with his pocketknife and took out the folded letter. Inside was also a check from a bank. "What now?" Ezra muttered with a frown. As he read, Ezra slowly shook his head, and his shoulders slumped.

Watching his reaction, Rose had to ask, "Is it bad news, Ezra?"

After folding the letter and putting it in his pocket, Ezra said, "Rose, do you remember Mr. Harlan DeWitt?"

"Oh yes," Rose said. "That man who had the gold claim in the Yukon with your pa."

Nodding his head, Ezra said, "The letter is from the attorney for Harlan's estate. Harlan died of a stroke a month ago. He left a will stating that his ranch and cattle be sold and the money be used to build a new library in New Ulm, his hometown, except for $5,000 he has left to me."

"Oh my lord," Rose gasped. "He must have been very well off."

Ezra sat down in one of the chairs by the stove, trying to absorb the news. "I had planned to visit him later this fall," Ezra said, shaking his head. "Now, he is gone."

Nathan came in from outside. "Is everything all right?" Ezra took the letter from his pocket and handed it to Nathan.

Nathan read it and then looked at the check. "We'll go to the bank tomorrow and deposit this," he said. "I am sorry about Mr. DeWitt; he seemed like a nice man."

Ezra took the letter and check, putting them into his pocket.

"I'll be here in the morning," he said, leaving.

CHAPTER TWENTY-SEVEN

"You're quiet this morning," Nathan said.

Ezra stared out the car door window, watching the farmland pass by. "It just doesn't feel right that people keep dying and leaving me money."

Nodding his head, Nathan said, "That does seem to be what is happening, but you put that money to good use, like helping add that wing to the hospital."

"Best money I ever spent," Ezra said, smiling.

Nathan's Dodge missed a beat, then settled down. "I think I need some new spark plugs," Nathan muttered.

"When we get to Burkesville, stop at the garage," Ezra said. "You keep driving me around and won't take any money. I'll get you some new plugs. I think I can afford it."

Nathan chuckled, and then both men started laughing.

At the garage, Nathan waited while Ezra spoke to the mechanic, and then the two walked to the bank. They asked a bank teller if Mr. Edwards was in. "May I ask who wishes to see him?" the teller asked.

"Tell him it's Ezra Mulvey." Moments later, the teller returned with Franklin Edwards. "What can I do for you this morning, Mr. Mulvey?" he asked. Ezra handed the man the letter and the check. As he read the letter, the banker nodded. "I take it you wish to deposit this in your account."

"I will need $200 for myself," Ezra told him.

"Sign the check on the back," Mr. Edwards said, which Ezra did. Taking the check and Ezra's small brown bank book, the teller returned moments later, handing the book and cash to Franklin. "You now have $10,400 in your savings," he told Ezra, giving him the book and the money.

Leaving the bank, Nathan asked, "Any other stops you want to make?"

Thinking a minute, Ezra asked, "You had breakfast yet?"

"Just coffee," Nathan said.

Pointing across the street, Ezra said, "Molly's Cafe makes good food, let's eat."

Lorna, the waitress, sat them at a corner table. She touched Ezra's shoulder and said, "I was so sad to read about Gina's passing in the newspaper."

Smiling, Ezra told her, "Gina told me that you helped her decide on a lawyer to draft her will. I thank you for doing that."

"She was a wonderful woman," Lorna said. "Now, what can I get you two for breakfast?" They both ordered bacon, eggs, home fries, toast, and coffee. When they finished eating, Ezra left a $50 bill on the table.

"That is one hell of a tip," Nathan said.

"She was Gina's friend," Ezra said as they left.

As they walked to the garage, Nathan said, "Rose and I

have often wondered, if Gina had lived, would you two have married?"

With a sigh, Ezra said, "Gina and I spoke of marriage several times. We decided many things needed to be worked out before that could happen."

Frowning, Nathan asked, "What things?"

Ezra stopped walking and turned toward Nathan. "Just things very private between her and I. That's all I can tell you."

Nathan blushed, looked at Ezra, and said quietly, "I asked because I care."

Smiling, Ezra said, "Just tell Rose we would have married."

At the garage, the Dodge was waiting. As Nathan waited while Ezra paid the bill, he noticed something different. Walking around the car, he saw all four new tires. When Ezra came out, Nathan pointed at the tires and said, "You didn't have to do that."

Grinning, Ezra said, "Driving me back and forth these past few months, those tires were getting pretty thin. Maybe I did it for my own safety."

Smiling, Nathan said, "Thanks, now get in, and we will try them out."

The garden was done. Everything had been dug up, stacked in the middle, and burned. Four stakes, each four-feet long, had been driven into each corner of the garden. Throughout the winter, the ashes from the stoves would be spread here as fertilizer.

Nathan had delivered a new woodstove the day before. The new stove was a Cleveland model. It was squarely built, standing on four legs with an eisenglass window. The old pot-belly New England stove had worn out or rusted out, and Nathan had hauled it away. A new stove pipe ran up and out the roof.

Ezra checked the chinking in the log walls, finding only a few places needing tending. The nights were getting cooler, no frost yet, but it would not be long before that became a regular morning sight. As he split more cut wood, Ezra smiled, thinking of Gina. She had loved his cabin, calling it her retreat. She had learned from Hannah how to make biscuits and was delighted with each batch she made. Her memory was like a sweet ache that never diminished. Tomorrow, he would visit Gina's Valley.

The valley seemed to defy the seasonal change. The colors of the flowers were as vivid as the first days of summer. The birches along the creek shone white as snow, with flashing green leaves. Ezra dismounted, unsaddled the horse, and left it to graze. He spread the blanket on the ground by the rose bush, the red petals open to the sun. New shoots were growing at the base of the bush, promising more flowers in the spring. A female cardinal flew in and landed on the lower branch of the old oak.

"It has been a remarkable summer, Gina," Ezra said. He went on to tell her about all that had happened. As he talked, Ezra opened his saddlebag and took out a sandwich and a bottle of root beer. As he watched, a male cardinal joined the female.

"Your friends are here," Ezra said with a smile. "I am glad they keep you company." The afternoon passed quietly, and soon it was time to leave. From his canteen, Ezra watered the roses, then said his goodbye. He saddled up and rode back down the path toward home.

'Evenings are cooler and coming earlier,' Ezra thought. Checking his Ingersoll pocket watch, he saw it was just shy of 6 o'clock. For supper, Ezra was having roasted grouse and squash. The new stove was working fine, and with the oven going, the cabin was warm. Two oil lamps were burning, one on the table and one by the bed. After supper, hot water was heated to brew a slow sup of strong coffee while he washed the dishes.

'Think I'll patch those jeans that wore out at the knee.' Ezra kept an old pair of worn-out jeans to cut patches from. Working at the kitchen table, he carefully measured and cut the patch, then cut away the frayed denim from the knee of the jeans he would fix. He carefully threaded a needle with black thread, rolling it off the spool until he thought he had enough. Turning the pants leg inside-out, Ezra pinned the patch in place and began sewing.

He thought back to the nights he had done this same thing for Micah. 'That boy was rough on clothes,' Ezra remembered fondly. Micah had asked him why he patched instead of buying new. "Waste not, want not," was Ezra's response. When he finished sewing the patch on the inside, he reversed the process, turning the pants leg back to the outside. Carefully folding the denim cloth in, he stitched the patch into the knee. When he finished, he held the pants up to inspect his work. 'Good as new,' he thought with a smile.

Ezra blew out the lamps, undressed down to his long johns, and went to sleep.

CHAPTER TWENTY-EIGHT

"I wish oak sawed easier," Eban said. "It might make this job more fun."

Ezra and Eban were cutting the last load of firewood to see them through the winter. A mixture of oak, maple, and pine was cut to length and loaded on the wagon. A bee buzzed past Ezra's ear, then another. Leaning on his axe, Ezra said, "Let's take a break a minute, Eban; I want to see where these bees are going."

"You think there might be a honey tree nearby?" Eban asked.

"Almost sure of it," Ezra said, "and I think I know where it is."

The two men laid down their tools and followed the flight path of another bee as it went by. "They seem to be heading for that old elm tree that got its top blasted off by lightning," Ezra said. Straight ahead was the tall stump of an elm with a ragged top. About six feet off the ground was a round hole, probably started by a woodpecker, then enlarged by either squirrels or possibly a raccoon. The bees had taken it over and built a hive.

"You think Hannah would like some honey?" Ezra asked.

Smiling, Eban said, "My mouth is watering; I am just thinking about what Hannah could make with that honey."

"I'll be here early tomorrow morning when it's still cold. Probably won't even need a smoker to get half that hive."

Walking back to the wagon, Eban asked, "Where are you trapping this year?"

"Just running a few sets on the south end of Otter Lake. Saw some mink tracks there," Ezra said. With the wagon loaded, the two men started for home.

It was still dark the following morning when Ezra drove his spring wagon into the Thorne's yard. Lantern light from the barn meant Eban was doing the milking. Hannah came out on the porch wrapped in a shawl. "Coffee is on Ezra. Come on in," she said. The kitchen was warm, and the smell of frying bacon greeted him.

"Eban says you are going after some honey this morning," Hannah said.

"Just waiting for it to get light," Ezra said. "I could use a bucket to haul it in."

Hannah handed Ezra the milk bucket sitting on the sideboard. Esther came into the kitchen, already dressed for school.

"Are you getting us some honey?" she asked Ezra.

"Yes, I am," Ezra said smiling, "and I expect one of your fine desserts."

Ester clapped her hands. "I will make you a fine dessert, I promise."

Eban came in carrying a bucket of milk. "You need any help this morning?"

"No thanks," Ezra said, "it's a one-man job." Through the window, the first light of dawn could be seen. Finishing his coffee, Ezra said, "Be back soon."

The temperature was almost cold. 'Right around 40 degrees,' Ezra thought as he drove up the lane. The first pale shade of yellow spread across the horizon as the sun rose. Ezra stopped the horse a few yards from the big elm stump. He took out a pair of leather gloves from his coat pocket and slipped them on. Lifting the bucket from the wagon, he walked to the elm. Not a sound could be heard. Holding the bucket in his left hand, Ezra eased his right hand into the hole in the elm until he felt the honeycomb.

Slowly, almost gently, he worked the comb back and forth until he felt it separate from the tree. Backing his hand out slowly, he set the honeycomb in the bucket. Ezra repeated this motion two more times, each time getting a larger piece of honeycomb. With his gloved hand, he felt how much comb was left. Satisfied, he eased his hand out of the elm. In the bucket were a few bees still in the comb.

'I'll let Eban worry about those,' he thought with a grin. Setting the bucket in the wagon, he backed around and drove back to the house.

Ezra's next stop was Herman Kruetzer's farm. Several men stood around a tall tripod, under which was a huge iron kettle full of boiling water. From the tripod hung the carcass of a gutted pig. As Ezra watched, the pig was lowered into the kettle. Steam rose and water slopped over the sides of the kettle as the carcass slowly sunk. Several men held round scrapers, ready to scrape the bristles off the steaming hide. Herman waved and walked over to Ezra's wagon.

"Mr. Mulvey," he said, "what is the pleasure of your visit?"

Tipping his hat back with his thumb, Ezra said, "I need about a dozen bags of straw for the winter."

His red face dripping sweat, Herman said, "As you can see, we are busy today. I can bring the straw over in two days."

"That's fine," Ezra said. "What will be the cost?"

Wiping his face with a large blue handkerchief, Herman laughed and said, "I owe you too many favors to charge you. Let it be my gift." The two men shook hands. Ezra watched as the pig was lifted from the kettle, and the men began scraping; then he waved and drove out of the yard.

Back home, Ezra staked the horses out in the pasture on long leads. The sun was working its way across a cloudless sky. It was warm, almost hot, with no breeze at all. Checking his snares, Ezra found only one rabbit. 'I'll put it on the outdoor grill,' he thought, 'two baked potatoes should do it.' As he cleaned the rabbit, a patrol car drove into the yard.

Sheriff Godfrey stepped out. "Got a complaint against you this morning," he told Ezra.

"Let's eat," Ezra said, "then you can arrest me."

Luther sat down on the bench next to Ezra. "Mr. Maynard P. Tuttle, who is hoping to be elected to the state senate, swears that you threatened to shoot him."

Ezra laughed. "Mr. Tuttle is about half right. He showed

up here demanding I vote for him. I ran him off, told him if he came back, I would shoot him."

Grinning, Luther asked, "You mean just to wound him a little?"

Thinking a moment, Ezra said, "Probably in the leg, or maybe a foot, nothing serious. Don't want no dead body littering the yard."

Luther began chuckling, then Ezra. Soon, the two friends laughed so hard that tears ran from their eyes. All too soon, it was over; the laughter slowly died as they gasped for breath. Finally, Ezra asked, "Want a root beer?"

"Just one," Luther said, "then I have got to go back to town."

"Give Mr. Tuttle my regards," Ezra said with a smile.

Old Elmer Whatley had died. It was not unexpected; Elmer was 79 years old with heart problems. His son, Lucas, ran the farm. Elmer spent his days in a rocking chair on the front porch, watching his son and grandson do the work. Lucas and his wife, Janet, had two children—a daughter, Linda, who was a schoolteacher in Cedarburg, and a son, David, who would take over the farm one day.

Elmer had died in his rocking chair. Lucas had made the arrangements for the funeral. Only a few were expected to attend. Elmer had not been well-liked; in fact, people tolerated him because they liked Lucas and Janet. It would be a somber affair.

Hannah, Rose, and Naomi Thorne were all members of the Ladies Aid at the church. They met at the store to discuss the luncheon after the burial. "Sandwiches, salads, and a dessert with coffee and cider to drink," Hannah said. "Naomi, can you make a cake for us?"

"I will make a devil's food cake and some cookies," Naomi said.

"We can make ham and cheese sandwiches at the church," Rose said, "and I will bring a salad."

"I will bake bread this afternoon," Hannah said, "and two jars of dill pickles."

"Janet said she can bring a potato salad and the cider," Rose added.

"I truly hope there is a good attendance," Hannah said, "out of respect for Lucas and Janet."

"I don't think Elmer had any real friends," Naomi said, "except for Ezra Mulvey."

"He respected Ezra," Hannah said. "How Ezra felt about Elmer, I really don't know."

After a bath and a shave, Ezra put on his best pair of denim jeans and a white shirt. He took a minute to decide, then put on a black vest, something he seldom wore. He put on his hat and went to the stable. He chose the chestnut to ride, cinched the saddle down tight, and mounted. It was after 11 o'clock, which meant the funeral service had already started. 'I'll say goodbye to Elmer one last time,' Ezra thought as he rode to the church.

Ezra arrived at the church just as the pallbearers were bringing the casket out the side door and loading it on a wagon. The cemetery was about 100 yards behind the church. Ezra tied the chestnut to a railing and followed behind. At the gravesite, the casket was lowered down, and the reverend began the prayer. Lucas Whatley spied Ezra and smiled. Ezra nodded back. The service over, the mourners followed the wagon back to the church.

Lucas fell in beside Ezra. "Thank you for coming," he said. "Pa would have liked that."

"He was always good to me and Micah," Ezra said.

Several men sat under the oak tree in the churchyard, sipping hot coffee and eating sandwiches. Ezra joined them, carrying a cup of coffee and a piece of cake. "Pull up some shade," Nathan said. "We were just talking about old Elmer. You got along with him better than anyone; how did you manage that?"

Ezra took a bite of cake, then a sip of coffee, and said, "I've got a story to tell that may shed a bit of good light on Elmer if you want to listen."

"Elmer never got along with any of his neighbors," Foley said, "something about his property line."

"I heard that too," Ezra said, "but my story isn't about that. It's about helping a neighbor."

"Everybody just hush up and listen," Eban said. "You might learn something. Go ahead, Ezra."

"It happened quite a few years ago when Micah and I were young," Ezra said. "We were out checking the trap line. It must have been a Saturday, or Micah would have been in school. On the way home, we sometimes took the shorter way across Elmer's woodlot. It saved us about a half hour's walk."

"Did Elmer know you used that shortcut?" Nathan asked.

"I don't think so," Ezra said. "We never used it that often. That morning, we were about halfway across when Micah stopped and said, 'I think I hear somebody yelling.'

I listened and heard it too. 'We better take a look,' I told Micah. 'Could be somebody hurt.'"

Esther came by with a big coffee pot and topped off everyone's cup. "There are some sandwiches left," she said, "but the cake is gone."

As she left, Foley turned toward Ezra. "What happened?"

"First, we saw the horse," Ezra said, "then we saw the man on the ground. It was Elmer, and he was hurt. He was hauling out two logs for firewood. He tripped on a tree root, fell, and one of the logs rolled over his left leg. He had dropped the reins, and the horse stopped right there." There was a silence as Ezra sipped his coffee and remembered. Finally, he said, "Elmer saw us and yelled for us to come over. 'Get this log off me,' he said. I told Micah to take the reins, and I lifted the log. It took all I had, but I did it."

"Was the leg broke?" Eban asked.

Ezra shook his head and said, "It wasn't broke, but his knee joint was dislocated. His lower leg stuck out at an odd angle. 'Can you boys get me home?' Elmer asked. I said we could if he could ride atop the logs. I took out the rope I carried in my pack and tied the logs together at the bottom, and then Micah and I carefully got Elmer on top. I picked up the reins and told Micah to see that Elmer didn't fall off. We took our time, and soon, we were back in the Whatley's yard. His wife, Gertrude, was still alive then, and she had Lucas get the wagon to take Elmer to the hospital. This was before they had an automobile."

"Did you go along with him?" Foley asked.

"No, we didn't," Ezra said. "Me and Micah went home, but two days later, Lucas came over and asked if Micah and I would come to Sunday dinner. I said we would; Lucas thanked me and left. On Sunday, we rode the old horse to Whatley's, and Elmer was glad to see us. He was getting around on crutches and had a brace on his leg. He shook our hands, thanked us for helping him, and asked why we happened to be there. I told him about the shortcut, and he laughed and said we could use it anytime. After that, I would stop in once in a while to see how he was getting on."

"When was the last time you saw him?" Eban asked.

"The day after Micah left," Ezra said. "I was using the shortcut, so I stopped by and told Elmer that Micah had joined the Army. After that, I kind of lost touch with the Whatley's."

Ezra's story concluded as Lucas Whatley stopped to thank everyone for attending. They all shook hands, and Lucas left. After the men took their cups back to the church, Ezra said goodbye and slowly rode home.

CHAPTER TWENTY-NINE

The sound of gunshots woke Ezra. He sat up, lit his bedside lamp, and checked the pocket watch he kept on the side table. It was five minutes after 2 a.m. Ezra dressed, laced up his boots, strapped on his Colt revolver, and shrugged into his coat. He opened the cabin door and looked out.

All was quiet. It was cold, being the middle of October, with a half-moon shining down. Ezra slowly walked to the end of his drive and checked the road. A dark shape was lying on the road to his right, about twenty yards away. Then the shape moved, trying to crawl toward him.

A weak voice called, "Help me."

Ezra moved toward the shape with his hand on his Colt. The shape was a man, and he was hurt. Ezra bent down and asked, "What happened?"

"I'm a state trooper," the man gasped. "I was chasing two men. They shot me and stole my car."

"Where are you hit?"

"In my left side and left leg," the trooper said, then quietly passed out. Ezra ran to his cabin and got the chestnut out of the stable. He harnessed it to the wagon and drove to where the trooper lay. The man was still unconscious, which helped as Ezra wrestled him into the wagon and drove to the general store.

Rose woke and shook Nathan awake. "Someone is pounding on the front door," she told him. Nathan mumbled something, lit a lamp, and put on his pants and shoes. As he came down the hallway, the pounding got louder.

"Alright, I'm coming," he yelled. He lit the lamp by the door and unlocked it. There stood Ezra, fist raised to pound again.

"I've got a wounded state trooper in my wagon," he said. "We got to get him to the hospital in Burkesville."

Rose was at the door now in her housecoat. Nathan ran to get his coat and bring his Dodge around. He parked by the wagon, and with Ezra's help, they laid the trooper in the backseat. "Rose, put the horse in the corral," Nathan yelled, then slammed his car door. Ezra was already in the car, so Nathan sped off toward town.

"Give me your handkerchief," Ezra told Nathan. Ezra leaned over the car seat, pressing his handkerchief against the trooper's side.

"How is he doing?" Nathan asked as he dug into his pocket for the handkerchief.

"The bleeding in his side is slowing," Ezra said. "Now I need to tie your kerchief around his leg."

"Where did you find him?" Nathan asked.

"I heard gunshots, so I went to check," Ezra said as he tied the kerchief around the trooper's leg. "He was lying in the road, told me he was chasing two men who shot him and took his car. Then he passed out." Noticing the trooper's empty holster, Ezra said, "They stopped long enough to take his pistol. Good thing I got there when I did."

Nathan stopped at the hospital's door. Ezra jumped out and yanked it open, yelling, "I got a wounded man. I need a gurney, NOW!"

A nurse came trotting down the hall, pushing the gurney. "Is he conscious?"

"No, he passed out some time ago," Ezra answered. Nathan and Ezra eased the trooper out of the car and laid him on the gurney. The nurse wheeled the gurney inside and hollered, "Call Doctor Nelson! We have a man with two gunshot wounds!"

"I am going to search his pockets to find out who he is," Ezra told the nurse. He found a wallet and badge in the inside pocket of the man's jacket. Looking in the wallet, Ezra told the nurse, "This is Corporal Norman Rosenthal, Wisconsin State Patrolman."

As if he had heard his name, Norman came to, looked at Ezra and whispered, "Thank you," and passed out again.

In the emergency room, two nurses were busy cutting away the uniform and cleaning the wounds. Doctor Nelson hurried in and took a look at the wounds. "I need his blood type ASAP; he is going to need more blood." Turning to Ezra, he said, "I remember you have type O blood. I may need you to donate." As he started to turn away, the doctor turned back and asked Ezra, "It wasn't you who shot him, was it?"

With a slight smile, Ezra said, "No, Doc, I'm the one who found him."

Looking at Nathan, Dr. Nelson asked, "What blood type are you?"

"I'm type B," Nathan said.

A nurse hurried in and said, "Mr. Rosenthal is a type O." With a slight smile, Dr. Nelson said, "Get another gurney for Mr. Mulvey, who is going to be our blood donor."

Ezra removed his gun belt, handed it to Nathan, and said, "Go down to the Sheriff's Office; there should be a deputy on duty. Let them know what happened; then you go home. And thanks."

Nathan left as Ezra was taking off his jacket and shirt. A nurse rolled the gurney in, and Ezra lay down. Looking over, he could see the doctor tending to Norman Rosenthal. 'It's going to be a long morning,' Ezra thought as the nurse stuck a needle in his arm.

By 7 am, Trooper Rosenthal was all stitched up and resting peacefully in a room. Ezra was sitting up with his shirt on when Doctor Nelson came to check on him.

"Those two pints of blood you gave probably saved Norman's life," the doctor said.

"How bad was he shot?" Ezra asked.

"It could have been much worse," the doctor said. "Both were straight-through wounds, no broken bones. He was shot with .38 caliber bullets, which leave a smaller hole than a .45 and do less damage."

Just then, Sheriff Luther Godfrey came in. "I no sooner got to the office, and they sent me here. What the hell happened?"

Doctor Nelson smiled and said, "Ezra, I want you to drink a quart of orange juice before you leave here to build up your blood, and thanks again."

Stepping off the gurney, Ezra said, "Luther, let's go into the waiting room, and I will tell you the whole story."

Ezra gave Luther Norman's wallet and badge and told him what had happened. "I will call patrol headquarters in Madison and tell them Corporal Rosenthal is out of danger and resting in our hospital," Luther said, "then you and I are going out to where the shooting took place. If two men took the Corporal's car, then their car must still be there."

"Might need a tow truck," Ezra said, "and it would help if we knew who the men being chased were and why the Corporal was chasing them."

"Let's go back to my office," Luther said. "Maybe I can get some information from Madison."

At the Sheriff's Office, Luther was on the telephone for almost twenty minutes. When he hung up, he told Ezra and two deputies, "Corporal Rosenthal was chasing two men who'd escaped from Stillwater prison in Minnesota. The men had a knife, forcing a local farmer to drive them to New Richmond, Wisconsin. There, they robbed a gas station, beat up the owner pretty badly, and stole a .38 Iver Johnson pistol that the owner kept in a drawer. They stole the owner's pick-up truck and drove off."

"Where does the trooper come in?" asked a deputy.

"Corporal Rosenthal was leaving a diner in Bloomer when the stolen truck sped past him. He gave chase, and the passenger in the truck leaned out and took a shot at his car. A Bloomer city cop saw the whole thing and called patrol headquarters. After that, they lost track of Rosenthal until I called them."

"Are they sending someone down here?" Ezra asked.

Luther smiled. "An ambulance is on its way to take Corporal Rosenthal home. I told them we would find the stolen truck and tow it to Burkesville."

"Stop at the store," Ezra told Luther. "I want to let Nathan know that Corporal Rosenthal is fine, and I also need to pick up my Colt."

Ezra and Sheriff Godfrey headed toward the four corners to find the stolen pick-up truck. With a sly grin, Luther asked Ezra, "Why is it whenever somebody gets shot you are somehow involved?"

"Just lucky, I guess," Ezra said. "Being an expert with firearms has its advantages." Both men laughed. "It would help to know more about the two escaped men," Ezra said. "Might tell us where they are headed."

"State patrol said they would send out pictures and information on the two," Luther said. "We should have it tomorrow." Luther drove up to the gas pump at the store. "I'll gas up while you talk to Nathan, but hurry."

Nathan and Rose were waiting when Ezra walked in. He told them Rosenthal was fine and on his way home. Nathan handed Ezra his Colt and asked, "How much blood did they take?"

"I gave two pints," Ezra said. "Left me a little weak, but I'm fine now."

The sheriff came in, paid for the gas, and said, "When we find the truck, we'll come back and call for a tow truck."

They found the stolen truck less than twenty yards from where Ezra had found the trooper. It was nose-down in the ditch. Sheriff Godfrey checked the gas tank. "It's empty," he said. "That's why they needed the patrol car."

Ezra opened the driver's door and looked inside. "Just an empty paper sack," he said.

"Let's call for the tow truck and wait for it at your cabin," Luther said.

"Good idea," Ezra said. "I'll make us some coffee and pancakes."

"Where do you get your maple syrup?" Luther asked as he dug into his second stack of pancakes.

"Three local farmers make their syrup," Ezra said. "This last batch is from Herman Kruetzer."

"Wish I had some bacon to go with this," Luther muttered.

Grinning, Ezra said, "Sorry, all out of bacon." Ezra filled their coffee cups. "My part in this is done, but I want to know if they catch the escapees."

"I should know more in a few days," Luther told him. "As soon as I know the whole story, I will let you know. By then, you should have more bacon."

A week went by without a word from the sheriff. Ezra had his wagon in the yard with the back end up on a block of wood and a wheel off. "The squeaky wheel gets the grease," he said softly. He dug some grease out of a gallon can with a flat stick and spread it on the axle, just as a car drove in and Luther and a man in a state trooper uniform got out.

"Ezra, this is Captain Louis Frost from Madison," the sheriff said. "He wanted to meet you."

The Captain stepped forward and held out his hand. Ezra shook it and asked, "How is Corporal Rosenthal doing?"

"He is recovering nicely, thanks to you," said the Captain. "I was told the blood you gave him saved his life."

"I just happened to be there," Ezra said.

"You are also the man who found him and rushed him to the hospital," the Captain said, "and when he is able to return to duty, he will be here to thank you himself."

"Would you like some coffee?" Ezra asked.

"I am pressed for time," the Captain said, "but thank you. I do have something for you, though." The captain took a blue box from his pocket, opened it, and handed it to Ezra. "On behalf of the entire Wisconsin State Patrol, I present you with this badge. You are now officially an honorary member of the state patrol." In the box lay a gold badge on a bed of blue velvet. Luther Godfrey grinned and slapped Ezra on the shoulder.

Ezra looked up from the badge and said, "Thank you, Captain. I will treasure this."

"Got some more good news," Luther said. "They caught the two convicts with a roadblock outside of Antigo. The Corporal will get his service revolver back."

CHAPTER THIRTY

The first snow of the year came in the early morning of November 1ˢᵗ – six inches of white powder that would probably be gone in a few days. Ezra woke before dawn, as usual, dressed, and stepped outside. The temperature was a crisp 25 degrees with no wind. 'Perfect morning to get some venison,' he thought.

Adding some wood to the stove, Ezra made coffee and took stock of his cupboard. 'Getting low on sugar and flour. I'll stop by the store later.' With two cups of coffee under his belt, Ezra picked up his Winchester and left the cabin. He saddled the pinto and took the trail east.

BANG!

The four-point buck dropped where it stood – shot through the heart. It had come down to the small creek for water. Ezra had been waiting for a half hour, knowing it would be there. With his rope around the horns, thrown over a tree limb, and tied to the pinto's saddle horn, the carcass hung steaming in the still air as Ezra dressed it out.

After washing up in the creek, Ezra laid the deer across the back of the saddle and rode to the Crossroads. Nathan was sweeping off the porch when Ezra rode up. "I told Rose you would be out hunting this morning," Nathan said with a smile.

"Let's get this fat four-pointer in and cut up," Ezra said.

"Take it out to my barn. I'll get Foley to help."

On top of a long table in the barn, Rose and Naomi wrapped the meat in butcher paper as the men cut it up. "This will make you some fine eating," Foley told Ezra.

"With a grin, Ezra said, "All I need is the backstrap and a roast; the rest is for you folks to split up."

"Rose, when was the last time we had Ezra over for Sunday dinner?" Nathan asked.

"I can't even remember," Rose said. "Ezra, will you join Foley, Naomi, Nathan, and me for a venison dinner?"

"It would be my pleasure," Ezra said.

"I will be baking a blueberry pie on Saturday," Naomi said. "I will make another for the occasion." The work went quickly, and soon, the packages of venison were taken in. Ezra got his sugar and flour, waved goodbye, and headed home.

On Tuesdays, weather permitting, several local women met to sew quilts. They took turns meeting at each other's homes. Today, it was in Hannah Thorne's living room. Hannah, Naomi, Rose, Emma Klein, Maggie Brunner, and Gladys Schwanke were working on a patchwork quilt that was almost complete. This quilt would be for Gladys – an anniversary present from the group.

Esther was learning how to stitch the patches together while Emma cut up one of Eban's old flannel shirts. "Who should we make the next one for?" Maggie asked.

Hannah's eyes brightened. "I would like to make one for Ezra Mulvey in memory of our friend Gina Forrest."

"That is a wonderful idea," Maggie said. "Do you suppose Ezra has an old shirt he could donate?"

"I happen to know that Ezra has a flannel shirt that Gina left him," Hannah said. "I am sure I can get him to part with it, as well as a few of his own."

"I would like to sew on that one," Esther said quietly.

"Indeed you shall," Rose stated. "Your stitching is as good as anyone here."

"How is Ezra doing since Gina's passing?" Emma asked.

"We just had him over for Sunday dinner," Rose said, "and he is just like the old Ezra."

"He will be here for Thanksgiving dinner,' Hannah said. "It would not be the same without him."

"There isn't a family around who Ezra hasn't helped at one time or another," Maggie said. "Bill and I think the world of him."

"He is and always will be a member of the Thorne family," Naomi said.

"When I see him next, I will ask Ezra for those shirts," Rose said. "He often stops by to see Nathan."

"Maybe he won't want to part with Gina's shirt," Gladys said.

"I say we tell him why we want it," Hannah said, "and this way, it will always be with him." The ladies all agreed this was a good idea.

The next morning, around 9 am, Eban and Hannah arrived at Ezra's cabin. Ezra opened the cabin door and said, "I just made a fresh pot of coffee. Come on in."

Hannah took a pint jar from her bag and handed it to Ezra. "My raspberry jam you like so much," she said.

"Thank you," Ezra said, "I thought maybe you came to see my new bathroom."

"That too," Eban said. "I always wondered how the rich spent their money."

Grinning, Ezra opened the bathroom door.

"It's wonderful," Hannah said as she inspected the tub, sink, and toilet. "Gina would have approved." Ezra blushed and nodded. Back at the table, they sat as Ezra poured coffee.

"I have a special reason for visiting," Hannah said. "The lady's quilting club is going to make you a quilt in memory of Gina. I know she left you one of her flannel shirts. We would like to have hers and one of yours to cut into squares to make our patchwork pattern if you would agree." Ezra took a sip of coffee and smiled.

"I have two shirts Gina left," he said, "and I have often wondered what to do with them. One is a blue and white check; the other is a red and green pattern. You may have both. Mine is an old black and green check, pretty faded by now." Ezra opened the chest at the foot of his bed and took out the shirts.

When he gave them to Hannah, he said, "I know Gina would love the idea of a quilt. Thank you, Hannah."

Hannah took the bundle. "I am going to round up all my quilters and take over the church's basement. Working evenings, we will have a quilt for you by Christmas."

The word went out to every farmer's family in the county. "We are making a special quilt for Ezra Mulvey in memory of Gina Forrest. We meet in the church basement." The women and their daughters flocked to the church. Groups were organized to stitch and cut squares. Some had to leave early, and some arrived late, but the quilt pattern began to emerge, and it was lovely. The men held their questions and remarks; some made their own meals and held their tongues. They had seen that determined look on their wives' faces before and knew not to interfere.

Hannah and Esther arrived home late on a Friday night. Eban and Daniel had done the chores, made supper, and put Jacob and Noah to bed. Daniel was finishing his homework when Hannah came through the door, followed by Esther. Their faces were glowing with pleasure.

"How is the quilt coming?" Eban asked.

"It is already half done," Hannah said, "and it will be the best work we have ever done."

"Everyone is getting along alright?" Eban asked. As with every community, there are grievances and disagreements.

"All old problems have been put aside," Hannah said, "and some old enemies are now friends again."

"It's almost like Gina is there with us," Esther said. "Everyone loved her."

Hannah nodded. "It's like Gina's spirit is there, watching us work." She sipped the last of her coffee. "Eban said when I first saw Ezra and Gina together, I knew that man had met his match."

As Thanksgiving Day approached, the work on the quilt stopped. All agreed to meet on the Saturday after to resume. It would be a very special Thanksgiving for the Thorne family. Daniel had shot his first deer. His first deer hunt with his pa was something the boy remembers all his life.

Just after dawn, a pronghorn buck had walked into the clearing. "Aim for the heart," Eban had whispered.

BANG!

Daniel levered another shell into the .30-.30 Winchester, but it would not be needed. With Eban's hunting knife, Daniel dressed the deer as Eban brought up the horse and wagon.

"You did just fine, son," Eban said. "We will have venison roast for Thanksgiving dinner." Together, they loaded the buck onto the wagon and drove home. Eban backed the cart up to the machine shed, and the deer was hung up. As they began to peel the hide off, Ezra rode into the yard from the lane.

"Daniel got his first deer this morning," Eban said proudly.

Smiling, Ezra held out his hand. With a firm grip, Daniel shook Ezra's hand. "Nice going, Dan," Ezra said. "Makes me proud to know you."

"You won't mind venison roast for the holiday meal," Eban said.

"Will Conner be here this year?" Ezra asked.

"He will be joining us," Eban said, "but his train to Brule River leaves the station at 8 pm."

"It will be good to see him again," Ezra said.

"If you give us a hand cutting this buck up," Eban said, "there might be some steaks in it for you."

Grinning, Ezra pulled out his knife. "Let's get to work."

Thanksgiving morning, Hannah's pa, Conner Lundtz, was the first to arrive. Daniel had been waiting to greet him.

"I got my first buck, Grandpa," he said proudly, "one shot through the heart."

Smiling broadly, Conner said, "I am proud of you, Daniel; you are one step closer to becoming a man."

Ezra rode in soon after, and the men were shooed into the front room while Hannah and Esther prepared the feast: venison roast, gravy, mashed potatoes, green beans, cornbread, pumpkin pie, apple cider, and plenty of hot coffee. Conner left early, "I have to catch the train to the logging camp," he said. "I will see you all in the spring."

Hannah prepared a bag of food for Ezra. "The quilt is coming along nicely. We are over halfway finished and will have it done by Christmas."

"I can't wait to see it," Ezra said. He mounted the chestnut and rode home.

This time of the year always weighed heavily on Ezra. He missed his brother Micah, but most of all, he missed Gina. In the evenings, by the light of a table lamp, he would read from the journal Gina had left him. She had truly loved him. It was there in her own words. Ezra welcomed the memories; they were a part of the life he cherished. He sometimes dreamed of their time together, of rides and picnics in Gina's Valley. Though the sadness of her passing had dimmed, his love for Gina grew, a timeless love that would never fade.

Two days before Christmas, Ezra stopped at the store. A rousing checker game was in progress. Foley and Rufus Dawes were evenly matched and taking their time. Rose was at the counter sorting mail. She motioned Ezra to one side and said, "The quilt is done! Now, the ladies want to present it to you right after the Christmas Eve service. Will you be there?"

Smiling, Ezra said, "I will attend the service with Eban and Hannah."

Rose giggled and clapped her hands. "A few ladies were afraid you would not be there."

"After all your hard work, it would be a sin not to show up," Ezra said.

"King me," Rufus yelled from the checkerboard.

"You got more luck than skill," Foley muttered. Ezra chuckled as he left.

The Christmas Eve service held an undercurrent of excitement and anticipation for the wonderful event to come. As the congregation gathered at the church, they knew another event was about to unfold. The candles cast a serene light around the manger scene, and the traditional Christmas hymns were sung loudly and clearly. Many eyes sought out the figure in the front pew. Ezra Mulvey, as he had promised, was there with the Thorne Family.

As the service ended, there was a slight shuffling of feet and a few whispers exchanged, but no one moved to stand and leave. The reverend motioned to Hannah, who stood and walked to the railing. She looked out over the people and began to speak.

"You all know me and my family, and we are proud to know all of you. Recently, our dear friend Regina Forrest, the county nurse, went to her heavenly reward. She touched all our lives, and all who knew her loved her. Our quilting club decided to honor her memory with a quilt made from articles of clothing she left behind." Hannah paused for a moment as Emma and Rose left their pews and walked to the rear of the church, then resumed speaking.

"Word spread across the county of our effort to complete this quilt by Christmas. Mothers and daughters packed the church basement and worked tirelessly to accomplish our goal." Hannah motioned to several women to come forward. Rose and Emma walked back to the front of the church carrying a large bundle. The women carefully unfolded the bundle to reveal what they had worked so hard to complete. The congregation gasped at the beauty spread before them. A patchwork quilt unlike any they had seen before. An array of every color known to man, and in the white center, the word GINA was spelled out.

One man began softly clapping his hands, and it swelled! After a few moments, Hannah quieted them down with her hands and continued. "If there had been time, Gina would have married our own Ezra Mulvey. Anyone who saw them together knew they were in love. With that in mind, we give this gift of love to the man she loved." The ladies gently folded the quilt and handed it to Hannah, who handed it to Ezra.

There were tears in his eyes as he accepted the quilt. For a minute, he was silent, then he spoke. "This wonderful thing you all have done will never be forgotten. Gina lives in all our hearts, and she is still with us, now, in this quilt. Thank you."

The women dabbed at their eyes, and the men barely held back tears. Then little Noah Thorne woke up, yawned, and asked, "Is it Christmas yet?"

As everyone left the church, Hannah asked Ezra, "Will we see you at church tomorrow morning?"

"If I don't sleep too late, you may," he said. "If not, I will be at your house for Christmas dinner."

The stars seemed especially bright as Ezra rode home cradling his quilt. Entering the cabin, he lit a lamp and laid a few pieces of hardwood on the coals in the stove. With great care, he spread the quilt over his bed. He blew out the lamp and went to bed. Sleep came quickly, and with it, a dream of Gina.

The End

ABOUT THE AUTHOR

Mark Gengler was born and raised on a small farm north of Medford, Wisconsin. He joined the U.S. Army in 1963 and was stationed at Fort Bragg, N.C., with the 82nd Airborne Division. He saw action in the Dominican Republic in 1965. After his discharge, he traveled America, working odd jobs in California, Texas, Colorado, Kansas City and New Orleans. He returned to Wisconsin and went to broadcasting school on the G.I. Bill. Mr. Gengler was a disc-jockey, got married, and went to work at the University of Wisconsin, Oshkosh, until retiring in 2003.

More by Mark Gengler

—

THANKS A LOT, GOD

– OUR ANCESTORS SERIES –

NOAH THORNE
A WISCONSIN FARM BOY IN THE 1920'S

WOLF CREEK CIDER
THE STORY OF AARON STROUD

MIGRANT!
THE STORY OF DANNY BROOME

MARSHFIELD 1919
THE STORY OF WAYNE SCHOOLEY

ORPHAN
THE STORY OF TYLER BRAUN

TRUE LEGEND
THE STORY OF EZRA MULVEY